I0726789

See You in Hell

DEMELZA CARLTON

DEDICATION

Sometimes you need to be an angel to get through a work day.
I've been lucky enough to work beside them instead.
For all those helpful angels who helped inspire this book and unleash it on the world.
For all my fellow commuters, corporate and civil workers. This one's for you

.

One

Job interviews were Mel's personal concept of Hell.

"So, why do you want to work here?"

"I don't," Mel replied.

Raphael sighed. "Come on, Mel. I'm trying to help you. In a real interview, like the one tomorrow, they'll ask you and you'll need a convincing answer."

Mel took a deep breath and tried to think of a reason. After a minute, she shook her head. "Sorry, Raphael. Ask me the next question. I'll have to think about that first one."

"How about telling them it's because you need the money and you've heard they have good pay and conditions? Or because they're the best in the business? Or because you want to make a difference in the world and they're the best place to do it?" Raphael persisted.

"I'll think about it," Mel said. "Try the next question. I still have a whole day before the interview. I might come up with something good by then."

"In your opinion, what's the worst thing about you?"

Mel stared at him. "What kind of question is that? I thought I was supposed to say things that make me sound good and employable, not let them know about my worst habits!"

"Don't tell them your worst habits. Say something that sounds good but that you don't like about yourself," Raphael suggested.

"I can't lie."

"Of course you can't lie – or you shouldn't. You need to say more than that, Mel. I know you've never had a job interview before, but you're not making this easy." Raphael ran a hand through his hair, looking worried.

"You're supposed to sell yourself."

Mel laughed. "Technically, this will be my first real job interview and my first paid job. I'd hardly call it selling myself. You make it sound so dirty…"

"Just think of something about you that's really desirable for the job, but that you might not like."

"My boobs are too big?" Mel suggested.

"Oh Hell…Mel!"

Two

"Good afternoon, welcome to Hell–"

Did she really just say that? Mel wondered, staring at the receptionist.

"–lth, Environment, Life and Lands Corporation. How can I help you?"

"Ah, I'm here for a job interview?" Mel left the statement hanging as a question – half hoping she'd be told there was no interview or vacancy, so she wouldn't have to undergo this ordeal.

"Oh, you're from the agency? Take a seat and I'll let them know you're here," the girl said, waving toward the uncomfortable-looking bucket chairs. She picked up the phone receiver and stared at her until Mel's nervous knees folded, dropping her onto one of the seats.

"Hi, it's Reception. I have an agency girl here who says she has an interview." The receptionist sniffed as if she felt the accuracy of this information was questionable. A pause. "No." The girl's chin pointed at Mel. "What's your name, agency girl?"

"I'm Mel."

The receptionist's shoulders slumped as her eyes implored Heaven for something she evidently lacked. Mel wondered if it was patience, good manners or the ability to smile, as the girl seemed to lack all three. "She says her name is Mel. Just…Mel."

Mel summoned a smile. She could be both patient and polite – evidently it was a rarity in this office, if the receptionist was anything to go by. Perhaps the girl was only a teenager, too young to know better, or maybe she'd had a bad morning…

"She's on her way," the receptionist said as

she clicked the phone into its cradle.

Mel considered asking who the girl was referring to, but decided not to bother. She didn't expect any answer from her anyway.

The door beside the reception desk opened and a red-suited woman emerged, scowling. She propped the door open with one shiny, red stiletto. "Melody Angel?" she asked, squinting at the sheet of paper in her hands.

Mel winced. "I'm Mel," she repeated, extending her hand to shake the red woman's.

She ignored it. "Follow me."

The woman turned to her right and entered a small meeting room. No, an interview room, Mel told herself, looking at the office chairs circling the table. The furniture was occupied by two men, a jug of water and some empty glasses.

Oh Hell. I hope all my practice questions with Raphael were worth it – and that I don't forget anything, Mel thought, attempting to keep calm. Please, don't let me stuff this up.

The door clicked shut behind her with a terrible finality as Mel took her indicated seat.

Three

"Why do you want to work for our company?"

Mel paused to choose her words carefully. "The Health, Environment, Life and Lands Corporation is experiencing unprecedented growth in a contracting economy, through turning the government push for cost-cutting, consolidation and privatisation into its primary strength. From securing contracts in health and immigration, to subsequent privatised government departments, the general consensus in the business community is that the Health, Environment, Life and Lands

Corporation will soon control all government services. That's unprecedented power for a private company – and I want to be a part of it, to witness its almost miraculous success."

The three interview panel members sported proud smiles at Mel's praise. The woman ran her fingers through her hair, giving Mel a glimpse of what looked like a small, pointed horn, before it was hidden from sight once more. Mel told herself she was imagining things.

One of the men cleared his throat. "What would you say is your worst quality?" He ran his tongue nervously across his lips and Mel could have sworn it looked forked.

"Three things," Mel replied smoothly. "A trinity, as it were. My eye for detail, my tendency to work too hard to the point of single-mindedness, culminating in my pursuit of perfection. I see things other people gloss over as unimportant and I work hard to ensure that my work doesn't include such errors of judgement. I'm a perfectionist – striving to provide the perfect product, even if I need to work harder to deliver that. That might be why

I have a reputation as a miracle worker." She blushed and lowered her head.

Beneath the table, she saw the tip of a pointed tail before it swung out of sight. She coughed to hide her exclamation.

"Would you like a drink of water?" the woman asked, filling a glass from the jug on the table. As she handed Mel the half-filled glass, Mel had the impression that the woman's fingernails bore an eerie resemblance to black claws.

Mel blinked and politely accepted the drink, sipping slowly. She set the glass down.

"How do you deal with working on multiple projects at the same time?" the second man asked. Mel strongly suspected the tail belonged to him.

She smiled broadly. "It's all about priorities. When I have competing deadlines, depending on my personal goals and those of my superiors, I assess my projects very carefully. They get allocated relative priority, based on their importance to both me and the people I work for. I then divide my attention accordingly. My time is valuable and wasting it would be a terrible crime, especially when someone else might need to pay for my oversight. The projects that are the highest priority take precedence." She couldn't keep the edge out of her voice and feared that the second man had noticed it.

His eyes appraised her and she caught a glimpse of red before they faded to brown once more. She resolved to be more cautious for the remainder of her interview. After all, she did want to get out of there alive.

Four

"Do you have any questions for us, or any further information you'd like to add?" the woman in the red suit asked. Her eyes had turned redder as the interview progressed, so Mel couldn't tell herself she was imagining things any more. Lilith – the woman's name was Lilith, Mel reminded herself. She couldn't remember the men's names.

"No, thank you. I believe I've taken enough of your valuable time today," Mel responded with a professional smile. She rose to her feet, smoothing her pale gold jacket and matching skirt.

The three interviewers stood with considerably less grace, making noises that expressed their gratitude for her time, for taking part in the interview, and for not mentioning the pointed tails beneath the table.

Lilith opened the door to release her, waiting for Mel to leave first. Mel stepped out and almost collided with a man in a dark suit.

His coffee splashed high, yet he caught most of it in his cup. Not a spot landed on Mel — just one on the man's shoe. "Damn," he swore, swiping at it with a black handkerchief that appeared almost instantly in his hand. As he rose from his crouch, he took in Mel's attire, from her toes to her raised eyebrows.

He summoned a smile that clashed with the stormy expression in his eyes. "I don't believe I've seen you in the office before, and I make it a point to know all of my staff intimately." He handed the dripping cup to Mel's haughty interviewer. Lilith took it without a murmur, even as some of the coffee slopped onto her shoes.

He held out his hand to shake Mel's. "Luce

Iblis, CEO of HELL Corporation."

Mel gave him her fingers, in such a way that he couldn't crush them in his firm handshake. "I'm Mel," she began.

"This is her first time here. She's being interviewed for a position here at Health, Environment, Life and Lands Corporation – as my executive officer," Lilith said.

Luce's eyes stared hungrily at Mel as she lowered her gaze. "Is that so? I suspect I'll be seeing a lot more of you very soon, then. I look forward to welcoming you to the HELL Corporation."

Mel caught the glance that passed between Lilith and Luce before the woman bowed her head in acquiescence. Mel lifted her eyes to meet Luce's, but smiled instead of saying anything in reply.

She felt his scrutiny follow her out to reception, where the red woman thanked her again and said they'd be in touch.

Mel tried to hide her smile as she left. Her stint in Hell was over for the day, and she hoped it would be her last for a long time.

Five

Mel waited on the station platform with all the other be-suited commuters. The train arrived, packed like a sardine tin.

A man behind her muttered, "I survived the London Tube every day – no worries getting on this!"

Mel stood aside for two people to squeeze out of the car before she sidled in, reaching for a metal pole to keep her balance when the train set off. A recorded message warned her that the doors were closing.

"Nope, not getting on this one," the Tube

survivor moaned as the doors shut, leaving him standing foolishly on the platform.

The train picked up speed rapidly and the man behind Mel almost fell on top of her. When he straightened up, she became far more intimately acquainted with the stranger's briefcase than she'd ever thought possible. She thought about accidentally stomping on his foot but decided that would only make the situation worse, because if he jumped, the briefcase would go up, too. With the corner of the briefcase jammed between her cheeks, she idly wondered what would happen if she farted.

Faintly, she heard a phone ring. The generic tone could have been hers, but if it was, she couldn't reach to answer it. Whoever it was would have to wait.

She sighed and closed her eyes. The stranger behind her sighed, too, sending a breath down her shirt to the lucky bra she wore on days when luck needed a little extra push. She struggled to maintain her equilibrium and vowed that if she felt the man's hand move at all, she was going to make sure the whole train knew he was a groper — and not the fish, either.

She didn't know how anyone managed an uncomfortable commute like this, twice a day, every single day of their career. Only an angel or a saint would survive without severely injuring someone in response.

The train stopped at the next station and the man with the penetrative briefcase got out. Seeing a spare seat, Mel took it, straightening her skirt as she sat. She took out her phone and started reading. She'd check her messages when she arrived home — she had no intention of letting the whole train know her business. Especially not after they'd all been unwitting witnesses to her getting a briefcase up the bum.

Mel lost herself in the book she'd picked up. Something about zombies and an Amazonian queen battling on the surface of Mars. Some people came up with the strangest things to turn into stories. She certainly enjoyed their efforts.

She felt almost relaxed again as the train arrived at her station and she trudged up the escalators so she could head home.

"Hello, Helpful Angels Agency. This is Persi. How may I help you?" her sweet voice gushed.

"Good afternoon, Persi. It's Mel, returning Raphael's call. He said it was urgent?" Mel tried to hide her curiosity. What could possibly be so urgent that Raphael had needed to call her before he knew if she'd left the HELL Corporation office?

"Oh! Oh, yes. Um, he's on a call – what do I do?" Persi giggled nervously. "I'm still not used to this switchboard thingy."

"You could put me on hold, or you could

tell me a bit more about what Raphael feels is so urgent. I've only been back from Iran for two days. I've spent most of that time either preparing for, or attending, today's job interview as a favour to him, when I was looking forward to taking some time off. I have so much washing to do and there's no food in the house." Mel could almost hear Persi's mind wandering. "How's your mother, Persi?"

"She's good. She's always good. Worried, though. The rumours say the old devil's working on another bid for power and no one's sure when he'll show his hand. They're saying he wants out of Hell and he'll do anything to get it." Another high-pitched giggle. "It's frightening, Mel!"

"People have been saying that for as long as I can remember and Lucifer is still firmly in Hell, Persi. I wouldn't worry about him. If he was marshalling all the forces of Hell for a takeover bid, we'd notice."

"But he's sneaky and this time's different, they say. He might…OH! The blinky light for Raphael's phone is off. That means he's free to

talk to you!" Persi squealed. "One sec and I'll –
" The beep of buttons cut off her voice before
it returned. "Raphael, it's Mel!"

"No, just me," Mel replied. "Did you hit the
flash key to transfer after you entered his
number?"

"OH! Thank you. Putting you through now,
Mel!" Persi said with another giggle.

A single beep, followed by some recorded
music – the unearthly sound of a string
quartet, Mel guessed. The music cut off after a
few seconds.

"Mel, you're the best and I need you,"
Raphael said. "You have to take this job."

Mel sighed. "I thought you just wanted me
to go in for the interview, to take a look
around and report back on my findings. Now
you want me to accept a job there?"

"We need an insider at the HELL
Corporation. They won the contract for
mining this morning. You've seen how they're
taking over. First the health and justice
systems, then environment, fishing,
mining…pretty soon, they'll control all of the
privatised government departments. We can't

let that happen."

Mel wet her lips. "Why me? Why can't you send an archangel in? I thought Gabrielle was due back from Russia any day. She's experienced and more than qualified. What about Michael? He's good with IT – he fits in anywhere."

"Gabi's still in Russia and Michael…he won't be involved in this one. It's too dangerous." Raphael didn't elaborate. His breathing crackled through the phone line.

"You're not selling me on this, Raphael. Too dangerous for Michael, part of HELL's biggest bid for power in millennia…I'm the last person you should tap for this one. You know I'm better in the background, managing from the shadows. I don't have a taste for danger like some of your guardian angels. I'm…"

"You're perfect," Raphael interrupted eagerly. "They won't suspect you because no one knows you. They'll dismiss you as a brand-new guardian. That's why we'll send you in as a new office temp, so you can…"

"An office temp? The errand girl who answers the phone, takes minutes at meetings and does the photocopying? Are you serious? Was that what I was interviewing for? They'll never buy it. I'm qualified to run their entire company, Raphael. They knew I wasn't an angel-in-training like Persi – from the beginning of the interview. I'm surprised I made it out of there safely." Mel shook her head. "Gabi, Mike…you should be sending in the archangels for something like this. I was planning on heading up to Korea…"

"We can't send Michael in and he knows Gabi, too," Raphael began, but didn't seem to want to continue.

Mel took the bait tiredly. "Who's 'he', Raphael? Michael's not afraid of anyone. After taking on Lucifer himself, Michael's not likely to get nervous around one of his deputy demons."

"We think Lucifer's in charge – directly, this time. If he appears in the office, you know Michael will pull out his flaming sword and all Hell will break loose. He'll set every demon he has against Michael. He won't let Gabi near any sensitive material, either. You're our only hope." Now Raphael sounded scared.

Mel blew out a breath, trying not to laugh. The CEO she'd met looked like he wanted her all over something sensitive – which had nothing to do with the Corporation. He couldn't possibly have been… "Lucifer. Out of the Pit and managing a company. Well, I guess I can't say I'm shocked. The whole place was full of demons in suits. The entire interview panel and their CEO, too. Look, I know demons are into the bureaucracy of contracts and such – they've been doing it since Roman times and they've gotten a lot better since Faustus – but surely Lucifer wouldn't be stupid enough to make such an obvious bid for power. It doesn't make sense." She thought of the arrogant CEO, passing his coffee cup to Lilith so he could check Mel out. The way Lilith had bowed her head, as if in respect – but Lilith was one of Lucifer's most trusted lieutenants. If the rumours were true, she was his mistress, too. Could the sleazy man truly have been the Lord of Hell? She couldn't tell Raphael that – what if she was wrong? She'd never had anything to do with Lucifer before and she knew very little about demons. Mel knew she needed to investigate further before she said anything. That meant returning to HELL. "Ah Hell. You think it's a serious attempt, if he's making it known he's involved, don't you?" She didn't want to believe it.

"That's why I need you, Mel," Raphael persisted. "If they think you're insignificant, they'll give you access to more than any other angel we send in. Being you, you'll see to the heart and soul of the matter faster than anyone else can. And…and you'll be well placed to take over the whole Corporation if it becomes necessary. Or get out quickly if he makes an appearance – so you can warn us. No one else can do what you can, Mel."

Mel felt distinctly uneasy. "Take over? You mean dispose of Lucifer? I don't kill demons, Raphael – you know that. Send in one of the Powers – you know this is more their area than mine."

If Mel couldn't hear Raphael breathing on the other end, she'd have assumed his silence meant he'd hung up. "We did," he finally said. "We sent in the twins – Camael and Samael. They were in the office long enough to learn that all the contracts between the Corporation and humans are watertight, before we lost contact with them. It seems they joined the HELL Corporation as part of a more...permanent arrangement. In their legal division."

"They poached our staff? Or is it worse than that? Raphael, if they're corrupting angels, I don't see how you can justify sending anyone in there. The risk is too high."

"Please, Mel," he begged. "You'll be fine. You're not as susceptible to corruption as any of the others. I'll bring in other angels to back you up as quickly as I can. The moment Gabi gets home, I'll send her to you, plus anyone else they'll take. The more power HELL gets, the harder they'll be to take down, and we have to stop them. We can't let Lucifer win."

Mel knew he was right, but that didn't mean she had to give in easily. Especially if it meant trading North Korea for Western Australia. The bulgogi was better in Korea, for a start, and there was something about the purity of fresh snow in winter. Hell would see snow before Perth did. "All right, Raphael. If they want me to work for them, I'll do it, but you'll owe me a huge favour."

"Oh, thank God!" Raphael cheered. "They already called to say you've got the job. They want you to start on Monday. I can email you the details, or you can write them down now if you like…"

"Send them through via email. I'll have to find something suitable to wear – it's been a long time since I spent any time in an office, and my luggage went missing between Tehran and home. I'm not sure where they sent my suitcase, but it arrived this morning, two days after I did, and it's full of sand. I think some of my underwear's missing, too. I'll need to do a fair bit of washing, in order to have a presentable work wardrobe."

"Thank you, Mel! You're wonderful – I love you."

"Yes, Raphael, I know. You're lucky I know you say that to all the girls. As long as you let me investigate this in my own way, we have a deal."

"Congratulations on your new job. We'll see you in HELL at nine on Monday morning."

Seven

They ended the call and Mel dropped her phone on the bench. Despite Raphael's confidence, she knew this would be her most difficult assignment yet. No angel had ever taken on the Pit and won. Every other angel had failed, corrupted into joining the demons' ranks. She wasn't just the best – she was the only one left. And she didn't have a thing to wear to work.

Maybe if she ironed some of her clean washing, something would look good. After all, it wasn't like she had to wear pristine whites like she did in Heaven.

"See you in HELL," she murmured, plugging in the iron.

Eight

Mel walked into the HELL Corporation building and took the lift up to the sixth floor. To her surprise, today's receptionist was a man. "Welcome to HELL. Can I help you?" he asked with a smile. He raised his eyebrows.

Suddenly nervous, Mel smiled back, keeping her eyebrows firmly down. "I'm here to start work. I'm from the Helpful Angels Agency..."

The receptionist's eyebrows lifted even higher. "I'll get her for you." He paused. "Yes, I have your angel. Did you want to come get her?"

For a moment, Mel thought he was talking to her, then noticed his almost invisible headset. Embarrassed, she looked out the window at the Christmas decorations in the foyer. It looked like someone had picked up some props leftover from the *Avatar* set and decided to use them for Christmas. In October.

A door opened and Lilith appeared, wearing a red pantsuit, an absent smile on her face. "Hi again, Mel. Call me Lili." She offered her hand and Mel took it. It was so cold and limp, she felt like she was shaking a chicken breast.

"Follow me," Lili said, swiping her card over the reader and opening the nearest door.

Mr Receptionist gave a wave. "Good luck!"

Lili led Mel through a maze in burgundy cubicle land. She stopped at one that looked no different to the others and gestured for Mel to take a red guest chair. Lili seated herself behind the desk, on an ergonomic chair that was just a bit higher than Mel's.

"Right, then. Here's all your pre-orientation training and checklists —" Lili pushed a thick folder of papers across the desk, "— and your login codes – you'll need to change the default password right away –" a single sheet of paper landed on the folder, "– and your desk is next to mine." Lili pointed over the partition to the cubicle next door, between the fire exit and a huge, concrete, structural pole. She smiled at Mel one more time before her eyes slid to her computer monitor in dismissal.

Mel stood and took a step toward her cubicle. "Ah, Lili, you never said what I'm supposed to do here."

Lili lifted her eyes. "First, finish your orientation, then we'll discuss tasks. You're an executive officer, which means you execute orders for anyone in the unit."

Mel looked down at the papers. "So I'll find out next week?"

Lili laughed. "You'll be done with that by the end of tomorrow. Read through the package today and tomorrow you'll be in the group orientation sessions in the training room. Most of the stuff is about safety – what to do if there's a fire. As if we'd ever have fires in HELL!"

Nine

Mel had been welcomed to HELL exactly six times since she'd arrived, ninety-two minutes earlier. The presentations had been so enthusiastically delivered that she'd checked her watch thirty-one times and tallied every welcome in her otherwise blank notes.

She felt like making a coffee, just to break the monotony, and it looked like the demons in the room all felt the same way. Two were playing poker, one was watching some sort of video on his phone, one was snoring slightly as she slept on the desk, and the remaining half-dozen demons looked like they weren't far off joining her.

The present speaker gained momentary life as her monotone became uncharacteristically animated. "And now, let me present the CEO of Health, Environment, Life and Lands…Mr Luce Iblis!"

The sleazy, coffee-spilling demon Mel remembered from her interview stepped in front of the projector.

"May I be the first to welcome you to the HELL Corporation," Luce began.

Mel carefully tallied a seventh mark on her page.

"I look forward to working closely with all of you, as we rise from our humble beginnings…"

Hell hardly had a reputation for humility, Mel thought idly. If Luce was a good example of the demon denizens of the place, arrogant beginnings seemed more appropriate. She glanced around at the other demons in the room, for she was definitely the only angel present. They all looked awake and somewhat attentive – or at least their eyes were open and facing front. Cards and phones had vanished.

As Luce droned on, pausing occasionally to deliver one false smile after another, she started to see the patterns. All the demons followed his words, laughing and smiling with him, as if they were afraid to even appear like they weren't listening. It wasn't so much loyalty as blind obedience, or fear. She began to understand precisely what she was facing – a united army who would serve their leader. A man who knew exactly what he controlled. She wondered whether they were quite as sycophantic when he wasn't around.

Her fellow orientees looked more human than the demons who'd interviewed her. There wasn't a tail in sight and they all had very human-looking skin tones. She had seen the occasional vestigial horn, hidden amongst hair, but she'd seen newborn goats with bigger horns. She'd had so little to do with demons in the past that she had no idea if their horn size and human appearance made them extremely junior or senior demons. She turned her attention to their leader, presumably the most senior demon.

"I'm sure it won't be long before the next time someone says, 'See you in Hell!' you'll wonder what department they work in and why you haven't seen them in the lunchroom here at work." Luce's teeth seemed perfect and white as he laughed loudly, joined soon after by his demon chorus.

Luce looked entirely human, Mel decided. Not a horn, hoof or tail out of place. Perfectly manicured nails that didn't make her think of claws. Yet no one could smile that much while their eyes remained soulless, black holes of hate – only a man who'd seen Hell every day for millennia and maintained his sanity. She had no doubts at all. This was clearly the Lord of Hell, she realised, as those dark eyes settled on her.

Mel shivered a little in her seat, in sympathy for how cold the man seemed. Was it the distance from Hell that made him so chilly, like some kind of fiery lizard? How horrible it must be to live such an emotionless existence – no happiness, joy or fellow feeling for anyone. She wondered how a man filled with such cold indifference could seduce so many angels to fall. All she felt for him was sadness. The danger Raphael spoke of seemed distant – she needed to know what this man planned and running off to Raphael right away wasn't going to get anyone anywhere. She needed to stay and observe for as long as she could.

"So, once again, welcome to HELL!" he boomed, with one last practised smile.

Mel regretted that she'd missed his speech while letting her mind wander, but the emotionless tone he'd used had made the words sound like he'd memorised them long before and not varied them much since. She vaguely remembered seeing a letter from the CEO in her notes yesterday – she'd probably already read the content of his presentation. The saccharine message hadn't improved any in his personal delivery.

"And now, we break for fifteen minutes to refresh and have a coffee!" the demon trainer called out. "Fifteen minutes on the dot!"

Mel slipped out to the kitchen so she could finally have a drink. Demons were known for their slavish devotion to Earthly pleasures – surely the rich, dark brew of office coffee would be one of those.

Ten

Mel carefully blew on her coffee as she returned to the lunchroom turned training room.

Luce reclined against the tiny bar in the corner, resting his arms on it so his hips were pushed into greater prominence.

Mel recognised his stance as one meant to draw attention to the bulge in his pants. The implied message was clear: the pants could be unzipped for the right girl or boy, if someone played their cards right. Mel had far more experience with such a stance than Luce probably realised – for she remembered a time in Russia when it had merely meant the man was rich enough to own a spare pair of socks to stuff in his pants against the frostbiting cold. Ah, Napoleon had been stubborn and arrogant, too, she recalled, but he'd been good for intelligent conversation. He'd also owned an ample supply of socks.

No one seemed game to speak to the CEO, so Mel took pity on him. Resting her elbow on the end of the bar, she asked, "Do you get bored, delivering the same orientation presentation every month?"

"Of course not," came the easy answer. "Every time I tell new staff about the achievements of the HELL Corporation, I see their pride in being part of my company, knowing the next team of new staff will be hearing about the achievements that they personally helped happen."

Mel laughed heartily. "That sounds like a rehearsed response if ever I heard one. Do you ever answer a question honestly?"

"Of course," Luce replied. Mel barely knew the man, yet she knew he was lying.

She pressed her lips together and gave a little smile in response, before turning her attention to her instant coffee. Attention it didn't deserve, but the muddy brew was an improvement to listening to the demon's rehearsed rhetoric.

Luce seemed to realise that he'd hit a wrong note. "It's Mel, right?"

"Yes," she acquiesced gracefully. "From the Helpful Angels Agency." A careful sip of coffee kept her eyes from meeting his as the cup hid her smile. She waited for the implied warning to sink in: far from being one of his demons, she played most emphatically for the other team.

"Ah. Ah, yes. I remember now. You're the new girl who's working under Lili, right?"

"I'm in the office beside her and I report to her, yes," Mel corrected. "I'm looking forward to seeing precisely which projects she has in mind for me. I understand the company's interests are quite diverse, so I expect the work to be different to anything I've done before, if nothing else."

"So what were you doing before deciding to

be my angel?"

Mel gave him her serene smile, knowing Hell would freeze over before she'd ever be his angel. He evidently didn't know that yet, so she replied, "Other temporary assignments, as required. I go where I'm needed, that's all." She took a larger mouthful of her cooling coffee, trying not to grimace at the taste.

"I'm sure I'll need you for something. Lili does a lot of work for me. She may even delegate some of her more delicate tasks to you, if you're lucky. We could be working very closely together on some of my pet projects." Luce grinned. "You'll want to make sure you wear a skirt." He stared at her pants-clad legs hungrily.

Mel wondered what he'd say if she admitted the closest he'd get to her was precisely where he was now – just out of arm's reach. She chose to say nothing. Instead, she smiled and nodded, then excused herself so she could wash the sludge out of the bottom of her coffee mug. She wanted to wash her whole body – the sleazy CEO made her skin crawl – but she hardly had time before the next orientation session resumed.

She slipped back into the training room, relieved to see that Luce had left. Somehow, she suspected she'd be seeing him again soon, though she hoped the opposite. Slimy snake of a CEO…

Eleven

Two demons crept into the room behind Mel, smelling strongly of cigarette smoke. Another demon inhaled blissfully. "Oh, that smells so good. I've been on nicotine patches so I don't have to go out for a ciggy, but it's just not the same…"

The trainer pressed some paracetamol out of the packaging and tipped them into her mouth, washing them down with her cup of coffee.

Mel glanced around – all the demons looked like they'd taken the opportunity to grab another foul coffee at the end of the break. Aside from a demon cracking open a can of Red Bull, she was the only one not holding a cup.

"Are we all back? Good. It's time to discuss our substance policy," the trainer began.

A demon sneezed, then blew her nose noisily. She pulled out some hand sanitiser and rubbed her hands with it.

A slide popped up on the projector screen. To Mel's mild irritation, the trainer read it aloud, as if the entire group were blind or illiterate.

"Our policy: No employee is to consume or use drugs or alcohol within eight hours of commencing work to start and/or return to work while under the influence of drugs or alcohol.

"The purpose of this policy is to maintain a work environment free from the effects of the use of drugs and alcohol. Therefore the use or consumption is strictly forbidden. The consequence of breaching this policy is instant dismissal." The trainer paused. "Does anyone have a problem with this?" She picked up her coffee and sipped it.

The demons shook their heads in unison. Mel heard some slurping their drinks, too. Demons. Oh, dear. This job was going to be much harder than she'd thought. If every demon in the place was as sloppy and slipshod as whoever had slapped together the substance policy, she had a lot of work to do. She'd best get started, then.

She sighed and said, "Yes. I do."

"Which part don't you understand? Or is it simply that you don't agree with it?" the woman asked, a superior smile on her face as if she'd be delighted to perform an instant dismissal.

Mel took a deep breath. "Well, the first sentence doesn't make sense. It looks like someone cut and pasted it but forgot to proofread it. Splitting it into two sentences might make it clearer. Ending the first sentence after 'commencing work', then replacing the 'to' with 'No employee is to start…' Admittedly, you'd need to define drugs and alcohol. It isn't clear as it is."

The superior smile widened. "I think our

policy makes it very clear. It encompasses use and consumption of all drugs and alcohol. No exceptions."

"In that case, all of us have earned instant dismissal in the last hour," Mel replied. "Including you. We've all had caffeine – coffee, Red Bull and the like – and then there's nicotine, paracetamol and just using alcohol sanitiser."

Laughter erupted behind her as the trainer seemed to choke on a coughing fit. "We didn't mean caffeine or those other things. Those aren't…you can't be dismissed for…" she spluttered.

"Under the wording of your policy, we can. What'll your CEO do when he finds out? Do you think he'll ban coffee or just decide to fire the lot of us?"

The demon's face grew an interesting shade of red and her horns appeared through her hair. "How dare you…He…oh Hell…he'll…" Anger shifted to fear in her face.

She must be terrified of the CEO, Mel mused. Surely only Lucifer could have that effect on demons. Mel smiled angelically. "I'd be delighted to help you reword your policy before he sees it. Perhaps if this orientation programme ends early, I'll have time today to help you before I'm expected back at my desk."

The trainer's face started to fade back to normal as she looked around. "Do you think…you might all go back to work without mentioning this? We can end orientation early, if you like…"

Every demon in the room rose and the orientees left quickly, with surreptitious, grateful nods to Mel. She returned these as politely as she could before she found herself alone with the trainer.

"You'll really help?" the trainer asked incredulously.

Mel beamed. "Of course. I'm an angel. It's what I do. Plus, I'm more than a little worried about what would happen if you banned caffeine from your office. I think Hell would be a happier place than here."

Twelve

"Ah, Lili? I'm done," Mel announced, relieved that she'd finally finished her orientation and all the getting-to-know-you sessions without giving too much away…and neatened up the substance policy so that everyone got to keep their jobs for another day.

Lili looked up from what appeared to be an engrossing email. "Done all your orientation? Great, let's get you a project." She reached for a stack of folders that threatened to topple over, picking up the yellow one on top. "Something easy to begin with. We need you to research rehabilitation techniques for graffiti criminals."

Mel felt her jaw drop. "You need me to do…what? I've never worked with criminals, rehabilitation or anything to do with justice before. Since when was the justice system privatised?"

Lili gave Mel a perfunctory smile. "After privatisation worked so well for the prison and immigration detention centres, privatising the justice system seemed the logical next step. It's the 'Life' in the name of our Corporation – Health, Environment, Life and Lands. Now, it shouldn't be a problem. Our Research Division has already written a report on this, so all of their references should still be on file."

Mel felt like she'd missed something. "If it's already been done, why do you need me to do it again?"

Lili leaned forward and lowered her voice. "Our Research Division looks at things…rather differently to us. We're not sure they took the research in the right direction. They may have focussed on art therapy because it was the easiest solution, as opposed to the best solution."

Mel laughed. "But surely art therapy would be both the easiest and best solution!"

Lili frowned. "Don't let their research blind you. Our Research Division has their offices next to an art school, which isn't the case with this office, so you shouldn't suffer the same bias as our head researcher."

Mel nodded knowingly. "Ah, an art school. Did your researcher have to do lots of research in the female life drawing class? I can understand why he'd advocate that solution."

Lili looked shocked. "You can't say things like that. Phil might consider it sexual harassment."

Mel wet her lips, wondering how to correct her mistake. "Well, it does seem like the first thing I'd think of. Drawing naked women would certainly have an effect on the minds of men in prison, particularly those who are already artistically inclined. Things don't change that much."

Lili's face lost all expression. "Sometimes they do, dear. Phil is gay and he's married to the principal of the art school, Lial. I understand the female form does nothing for him. You'll find he can get quite enthusiastic, describing the hard contours of a well-muscled, male body."

Mel felt her face flush. She'd forgotten that some men don't like women. She couldn't blame them – she was particularly partial to a well-muscled, male body, too. Admittedly, it had been a while since she'd been close enough to touch such a body, but she held out hope that she might, sometime soon…

Mel shook herself. This wasn't the time to think about sexy men. She had work to do and any attractive men on her horizon would have to wait until she was finished with her current assignment. Or until she'd at least earned a holiday from it.

"Well, I guess I'll get started then," she said with false cheer, picking up the yellow file and walking away as quickly as she could.

She sat at her desk and restrained herself from banging her head repeatedly on the laminated surface. She resisted searching the Internet for images of hot men – she knew where that would lead, though the kitten photos that came up were always cute. Instead, Mel took a deep breath and got to work, not lifting her head until the day was done.

Thirteen

When Mel returned from lunch, a small sheaf of papers covered her keyboard. The words, 'NOT complimentary!' were scrawled across the front page in red ink.

She eyed it for a moment and decided that the red pen scrawl over the front of the memo she'd sent was definitely not complimentary, to the point where she considered it quite rude. She took a closer look at the pages.

On the second page, the red ink surfaced again, carving a ring around the word 'complimentary'. She took a deep breath as she decided that the red-pen wielder didn't like the word. Perhaps they'd prefer something insulting instead?

"…this initiative will be complimentary to our efforts to rehabilitate car thieves and graffiti artists…" she read.

What's wrong with saying nice things about their efforts at rehabilitation? Mel wondered. It wasn't her line – someone up the chain of command had tainted her text with bigger words and, apparently, mistakes, too.

She decided to ask Lili.

Lili laughed when she read the papers. "Ah, the Luce red pen of doom. It's your turn this week."

Mel was confused. "My turn? This isn't even my mistake!"

"Like an impotent man's used condom, our CEO's ego needs reinflating from time to time, usually at least once a week. Last month, before you started, Luce sent out a rant about how many people confused compliments with complements. Something about the first one saying something nice and the second one 'completing me' or some shit like that. You're the first one to make the mistake after his rant, so you get to apologise." Lili didn't look sympathetic.

Mel's confusion deepened. "Apologise? For not getting his email before I started working here and fixing someone else's mistake after this left my desk? Shouldn't the person who made the mistake be doing this, as they did get the email?"

"You're forgetting that whoever did make that mistake is higher in the company hierarchy than you are, and we'll all delegate the letter to you anyway, whether it was your mistake or not." Lili shrugged. "Hey, it's better than getting his email, ignoring it and having to explain why. At least you have an excuse. Just write up another memo apologising for the mistake and he'll forget about it as soon as he feels his ego is swollen enough again."

"I have to write a formal apology?" Mel was mortified. "Can't I just pull the original memo, fix the mistake and resubmit it?"

Lili smiled. "Sure you can, but that puts your memo at the bottom of the pile, which means it'll be delayed by at least another week or two. Then you'll have to write a memo apologising for the delays to your project instead." She shrugged. "Think of it as one of those, 'Other duties as required,' on your job description. You do what you're told and you get paid for it. At least he's not asking for you to do it on your own time, or when you had leave booked!"

Nor was he asking her to personally deliver her apology to his office, where she'd have to dodge his sleazy advances, Mel consoled herself.

She sighed and returned to her desk. The CEO of HELL threw tantrums that would embarrass a two-year-old because he didn't like someone's choice of words and he had an ego the size of a hot air balloon, which deflated rapidly in the chilly corporate atmosphere. So it was no different working in HELL than anywhere else. She took a deep breath and started wasting her afternoon on stroking the CEO's ego. At least that was all she was expected to stroke.

Fourteen

"Yep, that looks fine," Lili said, pushing the piece of paper across the table to Mel. "Just change it to the font in the style guide and you can take it up to Luce yourself."

"I…what? I thought you said I just had to write it and send it up to him," Mel protested.

Lili's eyes glowed red as if she sensed Mel's discomfort and enjoyed it immensely. "Oh, no. He came down here personally and placed the offending report on your desk. He waited a while, too, determined to make sure you understood his message. He insisted that I send you to report to him as soon as you received it."

Mel felt her jaw drop. "But…that was hours ago!" She felt her stomach and the sandwich inside it start to sink.

Lili grinned fiercely. "Then I suggest you change the font quickly and leg it up those stairs to Luce's office before you're any later."

Struggling not to swear, Mel marched back to her desk to make the letter and offending memo as perfect as she could. Fifteen minutes later, she pulled the pages from the printer and set off for the executive suite upstairs.

She kept a serene smile on her face as she strode through the maze of cubicles, nodding slightly every time she caught the eye of another demon. She'd never recognise them all, but it still seemed a good idea to stay on good terms with them. If her job survived the day and the belated dressing-down from Luce.

She shrugged. If her first job lasted less than a fortnight, so be it. She didn't much like the work, anyway, and there were plenty of demons to do it. It's not as if the HELL Corporation would miss her. She'd tell Raphael that the CEO definitely was Lucifer and let him sort it out while she went to Korea. She could taste the bulgogi already…

The cubicles were bigger now – spacious enough to take several visitors and a large meeting table between them. Mel knew she was nearing executive territory.

"Can I help you?" an imperious voice asked. Mel heard the words, along with the implied message that the owner of the voice would not help her. Mel was perfectly happy helping herself.

Mel's smile lit up her whole face. "Lili sent me to see Luce regarding a report." She proffered the papers.

The older woman's lips pursed as her deep, dark eyes narrowed. She had to be one of Luce's more senior demons. Her demeanour spoke of indescribable age and experience – all of it decidedly dark.

"I'm Mephi, Mr Iblis' personal assistant," the woman said, emphasising the demon's name. "All of his appointments go through me. Do you have an appointment?"

The woman's subtext was amazing, Mel

decided. She radiated an aura that said Mel hadn't a hope of getting through her and she'd never be important enough for an appointment. Despite herself, she was impressed. She wondered how many demons balked at this formidable gatekeeper.

"I'm delighted to meet you, Mephi. I wish I'd known to call you first – but Luce left this on my desk and insisted I speak to him about it immediately. Given the urgency, I didn't dare delay." Mel let the slightest look of concern cross her face. "I haven't missed him, have I? I'll wait as long as I have to, if he's with someone. I'd hate to be the one responsible for this getting to him later than he'd like." She slipped on a sympathetic smile that suggested she wouldn't want Mephi to bear the brunt of her boss's wrath.

Mephi held Mel's gaze for a few seconds before she conceded her point and picked up the phone. "Mr Iblis, I have an angel here to see you." She managed to make it sound like something she'd found floating in the staff toilets.

"If you're talking about the girl standing at

your desk with the papers in her hand, send her right in, Mephi," came a voice from behind Mel.

Mephi shrugged. "If you say so," she sniffed, clicking the phone handset back into place.

Mel nodded her thanks to Mephi with an unwavering smile, before turning to brave Luce in his lair. His office, she corrected herself, as she entered the airy space. She couldn't imagine a lair containing…

"Are those Pro Hart landscapes?" Mel asked eagerly. "I don't think I've ever seen the originals in oil before – just prints of them. It's the colours. They're always so vibrant, so real…"

"They are," Luce replied, "but you're not here to discuss my art collection. You've kept me waiting and I am far from happy." His eyes seemed to catch the light in odd ways, as if each was a singularity drinking the photons in, with no intention of releasing them.

Mel stepped forward and laid her papers on his desk. "The corrections you requested, along with a letter."

Luce gave the papers a cursory glance before turning the full pull of those dark eyes on Mel. "Do you know how long you've made me wait?" He lifted his chin. "Close the door."

For the first time, Mel felt a premonition of danger. The demon reclined in his desk chair with his hands in his lap, a picture of relaxed repose. Only his eyes seemed to belie the image – like a crocodile lurking beneath still, muddy waters. Did the crocodile know how much danger he was in?

"No," Mel said.

Fifteen

Luce snorted. "I can have you naked on the desk with the door open or closed. It makes no difference to me. You might be embarrassed later if Mephi hears you moaning, though, which she won't when you close the soundproof door."

Mel struggled not to laugh. She even swallowed her smile before she spoke. "And I can have you up on sexual harassment charges before you can get your hands out of your pants to zip them up. If you'd wanted to see me sooner, you should have left a written note or emailed me, instead of leaving a message with Lili. She only told me a few minutes ago that you wanted to see me." The sounds of furtive zipping confirmed what had only been a guess. "Do you want me to turn my back and wait a minute, while you finish putting your bits away? I wouldn't want anything getting stuck or hurt, with you rushing things and all."

To hide the laughter still threatening to escape, she turned and kicked the door shut. This demon wasn't dangerous – he was ridiculous, she decided.

"Now strip and get your arse on the desk," Luce instructed.

Mel stared at him. He couldn't be serious, could he?

"Every other girl in this building knows how to do as she's told. Do you know how many girls I've had on this desk? You should consider yourself lucky. The last one I had in here was so quick getting undressed that I managed to give her a full fifteen minutes of my time. At this rate, you'll be lucky to have five."

Mel became transfixed by the timber

desktop. "Did you wipe it clean afterwards?"

"What?" Luce's face reddened.

"Did you wipe it clean afterwards?" Mel repeated patiently. "I mean, you work on it every day and my report's there now. At the very least, I'd give it a good spritz with the Spray and Wipe and some paper towel before I used the desk again for work. Imagine how many diseases and strange germs each of your, er, accommodating staff members contributed when they placed their bare behinds on your desk."

The shock on Luce's face was priceless. He edged his chair away from the suddenly suspicious surface.

"Did you want me to go ask Mephi if there's a bottle in the kitchen?" Mel offered. "I'm sure I could wipe your desk down for you, just this once, if it makes you feel uncomfortable. We can get the cleaners to include that as part of their regular evening duties, if you like." She coughed. "Ah, you might want to zip up that last inch first…" She glanced away and heard the squeal of a quickly fastened zip. "There. That wasn't so hard, was it?"

A second too late, she realised her poor choice of words and it was her turn to blush.

Luce exploded with laughter. "You have no idea. I'm still trying to work out whether I should remind you that I can fire you if you don't do what I say, but something tells me you know that already."

Mel shrugged. "Sexual harassment and unfair dismissal. You'll be on a roll with the Equal Opportunity Commission with those two. You'll have a trifecta with the occupational health and safety risk of that unhygienic desk."

"It'll be my word against yours," Luce replied. Dark eyes seemed to bore into hers and Mel gave in to curiosity, looking deeper into a darkness that seemed too dense to be true. Did the demon have a soul under that thick layer of shadow, or was that miasma all that was left of his soul? Was his apparent humanity just an illusion?

Mel dropped her voice. "Everyone knows that angels don't lie, but demons do." She held his gaze until he closed his eyes, revealing nothing more.

"You've got balls, angel."

Mel lowered her eyes. "Actually, I don't, but we're not going there. I don't do demons, Luce. I gather there are some girls who like being ordered around like unpaid prostitutes, but I'm more of a dinner, flowers, chocolates and gradual sort of girl. And I really do prefer wings to horns." Her smile was apologetic. "Do you want to discuss my report? I believe the spelling mistakes were inserted by Lili or someone else who altered the document after it left my desk. I agree that my reports shouldn't have spelling mistakes in them, hence the present one is as near-perfect as I can make it."

Luce waved his hand dismissively. "I'm sure the report's fine now. Leave it with me."

"The only thing you wanted to discuss was whether I'd sleep with you?" Mel asked.

Luce seemed surprised. He evidently wasn't used to forthright angels, Mel mused. Perhaps she should have been more careful – or at least less frank.

"Not so much sleep. I definitely want you awake." He paused before adding, "Look, I lied."

Big surprise there, Mel thought.

"When I said I'd only have five minutes for you, that's not true. I don't have any more meetings or appointments today. You can have me for as long as you want. All night, if you like." Another pause. "And it doesn't have to be the desk. There's this chair, or up against the wall, or on the floor…or even on the couch!" Luce sounded really proud of himself. "I'll tell you what. I'll even let you choose."

Mel felt a stab of pity for the man. He had no idea how wrong this whole conversation had been. "Thank you for the truly tempting offer," she began carefully, "but I'm going to have to refuse. I have plans tonight and I'm just about to finish work for the day."

His grin faltered, as he looked shaken. Mel's heart ached in sympathy. "Well, if you're sure…maybe another time, then."

Mel managed to smile politely before making as dignified an exit as she could.

As she reached the stairs down to her floor, she clearly heard him say, "Shit!"

Indeed, she thought, remembering that her

plans tonight included stopping at the supermarket to pick up some toilet cleaner on her way home so she could clean the porcelain receptacle. It's not like she'd lied to him about having plans…

Sixteen

There was something oddly satisfying about a freshly-scrubbed toilet. Perhaps it was the way the reflective white porcelain shone. Or maybe it was simply the knowledge that it would be a whole week before she had to inhale bleach fumes again.

"Mel? What's for dinner?" she heard Raphael call.

There was a surprise. He'd wandered in and let himself in with the spare key without telling her he was coming. Had he heard about Luce's ill-conceived attempt at seduction already?

She found Raphael in the kitchen, chugging a beer. "Ooh, I haven't had one of those in a while," she said. "Are there more in the…thank you." She took the open Rogers and smiled as she sipped from the stubby. "So, did you bring me dinner, too?"

Mel registered Raphael's shock and laughed. "If you want me to cook dinner for you, you'll have to call in advance to let me know. I've been running around after demons all day and I'm done for. I was going to make a sandwich or head up to the little Japanese place by Canning Highway. Take your pick and we'll do it."

"How about I go pick up some Japanese and bring it back here? Tempura and tofu?" Raphael offered.

Mel smiled. "If you're offering to buy me dinner with all the extras, you're going to be asking for another favour before the night's out. I shall sit here, drink my beer, and wait for you." She settled on the sofa, bottle in hand. It looked like the neighbours' kitten had sneaked in and curled up on her desk shelf again. The tiny creature would've fitted on a saucer with space to spare. She decided to let it sleep for a bit longer before she carried it home to its owners.

Raphael left and returned with their bento-boxed dinner. Mel used his absence to set the table with chopsticks and condiments, before brewing a pot of traditional Japanese tea.

After slurping artfully at his udon, Raphael paused to wipe his face with a napkin. "How's work?" he asked, fishing for more noodles with his chopsticks.

"I spend all day doing random tasks for demons. If I told you half the pointless things they make me do, you wouldn't believe it. My reports have to be perfect and approved by my superior, Lili. Then she sends the document up to the person she reports to, who makes any changes they want, who then sends it further up the chain for everyone else to do the same…until it ends up on the CEO's desk for him to approve for release. If the CEO likes it, great, but if he decides that one of the commas inserted by someone along the chain isn't where he wants a comma, the report is dumped on my desk with a nasty note or, worse, a demon in person, demanding to know why I'd make such a mistake and insisting I fix it immediately. If I don't, I'm assigned some even less appealing task to do on top of my existing workload…" She wondered if she should tell him exactly what Luce had ordered her to do, but it'd probably shock poor Raphael.

"I would believe it. It sounds like the old government approval process the demons inherited when they took on the contracts. Humans can be even more bureaucratic than demons where government business is involved." Raphael transferred what looked like a piece of chicken into his mouth, followed by more noodles and a big slurp of broth. "Any sign of Lucifer yet?"

Mel hesitated. She was certain the CEO was the Lord of Hell. It felt too far-fetched, though. What could Lucifer possibly want with Western Australia? Weren't there more populated places he should look to conquer first? She wanted more time to find out what he was up to before she left HELL. But she had to say something – Raphael expected a response. "What does he look like? I think I might have seen him once, ages ago. I'm sure his time in Hell has changed him since then."

Raphael shrugged. "We have no idea what he looks like. He changes his form more often than humans today change clothes – he's so good at it, he could pick exactly what would best attract a human. Even as an angel, he was like that. Now…Hell, he could be anyone. Look like anyone. It's his soul you'd recognise. Once you know him, it's hard for him to hide. He has the blackest, most corrupt soul of any demon I've ever met. Charming to a fault, always looking for a way to seduce you to do exactly what he wants. Using any means necessary. Be glad you've never met him, Mel. He's not someone you want to go up against."

"But that's why I'm there, doing whatever menial office tasks his minions come up with, isn't it? To spot him and take over from him?" Mel asked, selecting another piece of tofu.

"NO!" Raphael dropped the clump of noodles back into his bowl so suddenly it splashed soup across the table. "If you spot him, get out and tell me. He's dangerous.

Avoid him at all costs, Mel. Do you know what he'd do to you if he knew who you were and what you can do?"

Mel smiled. "I'm Melody Angel, an office temp who can photocopy a few thousand pages without swearing when the photocopier gets its seventeenth paper jam. Who can answer the phone politely and transfer calls when I get a dozen misplaced calls that should have gone to Reception, some demon or even a building company in Osborne Park with an almost identical number to mine. Raphael, honestly – he'd probably just offer me a permanent job as his office assistant." She laughed. "To be honest, that's not a bad idea – I'd be well-placed to see everything that goes on and…"

"That's not a joke, Mel. He offered Camael and Samael jobs in his legal department and now I can't get them to take my calls or even speak to me. If he offers you a job, promise me you won't take it. Please, Mel!"

Mel had never seen Raphael look quite this scared. "First, tell me what you haven't yet."

"I promised…*I swore*…" Raphael stammered.

"You owe me more than that," Mel said, her voice deceptively soft. "You will tell me why. What danger does Lucifer pose to me alone?"

"He'll take you to Hell with him. Michael saw it. If he ever gets close enough to you to ask for your help, he won't let you go. Your destiny will be to descend into Hell with him."

Mel's voice dropped lower. "When did Michael see this?"

Raphael swallowed. "Before…before the battle when Lucifer fell. Michael swore he'd win, so he could keep you safe. He asked me to help hide you from Lucifer in any way I could. I've tried – for centuries, I've tried! – but none of us, not even Michael, expected him to take over HELL Corporation personally. And here, of all places, where I know you keep a permanent house to stay in when you're on one of your sabbaticals. I had no one else here to ask – but I don't want you to take any unnecessary risks." He stared at her, as if weighing his guilt. "Please, Mel. None of us wants to see you in Hell. Is there anyone you've seen at the HELL Corporation that you might think is Lucifer?"

Mel sighed. "The CEO might be. I don't know the demon at all. He goes by the name Luce Iblis. Look, it's only a suspicion – the attempts I've seen him make at seduction weren't the sort to be successful. They were just plain sad. The man's definitely a demon of some kind, but Lili seems a far nastier piece of work. Get Gabi here. She'd be able to recognise him, if he is indeed Lucifer. And if not…well, at least I'd have some help around the office. The photocopying is tedious, to say the least."

"Yes! I'll call Gabi in the morning. We can't be too careful. It could just be a ploy to get you to drop your guard after all. She'll help you in any way she can. I swear it." Raphael slurped up the last noodle and grinned as he set his bowl back on the table.

Mel raised her beer in a toast. "To a better day tomorrow, then," she said. After all, it could hardly be worse than today.

Seventeen

"It's Gerry's birthday on the weekend and we're all putting in to get him a present," announced Merih. "What does everyone think about a new tablet and a mankini?"

Mel thought it would be quite expensive, but she didn't say so. She also wondered why Gerry's manager wanted him to have a mankini. She assumed that was a matter between the two of them.

Merih's eyes swept the room. "So we're agreed, then?"

Some heads nodded slowly. Merih's eyes

darted to each member of the group before fixing on Mel. "I'll take care of the tablet. Mel, could you arrange a mankini?"

Mel was taken aback. Why would she know where to get a mankini? "I wouldn't know where to start. I've never bought one before." She'd be content to never buy one at all, nor see one on any man she knew.

Merih laughed. "Ah, you'll be fine. I'll leave it to you. We need it for tomorrow, so hurry up!"

Mel saw Lili nod, smiling, so she resigned herself to the task. Executive officers execute orders, she reminded herself.

She sat at her computer and searched for mankinis. She discovered that they used to come as a free gift with Borat DVDs, but not any more. There were plenty on eBay, but there was no way she'd have it by tomorrow. All the other hits were pictures of men who owned a mankinis – one had huge tufts of black hair sticking out of it – or ads for sex shops.

She opened up tabs for a few and steeled herself for unpleasant research. She let out her breath in a relieved hiss as she clicked on the first page. It featured a warning message, telling her the page had been blocked because it might contain pornographic content.

It's a sex shop, Mel thought. Of course it might contain pornographic content.

She clicked on the web address again, but the site was still blocked. She tried the next and the next…but they were all blocked. She jumped up and trotted over to Lili's cubicle.

"Ah, Lili?"

"Mmm?"

"I can't seem to find a mankini online, because the sex shops are blocked." Her voice carried over the cubicles and some heads popped up to glance at Mel before slowly shrinking out of sight.

"You can't look at sex toys at work," Lili whispered.

Mel was both annoyed and confused. "But don't we regulate prostitutes and brothels?"

Lili gave her the smile that made Mel feel stupid. "Yes, but not adult shops." She kept her voice low. "I guess you'll just have to go out to one and see what they have. Ring them first, though."

Mel lowered her voice to match Lili's. "I don't know where they are. I've never been into a sex shop. I wouldn't know what to ask for."

"Oh, the nearest one is on Murray Street," Lili said dismissively. "It's called XXX or something. Their number should be in the phone book – ring them and I'll escort you there so you don't get lost."

Mel rang the number on the phone book's website and explained to the chirpy woman on the phone what she was after.

"Oh, we have them in several colours. Which would you like? They're part of the Bang Him range, sweetie." Mel wondered if the woman was testing out the merchandise under the phone desk, she sounded so cheerful.

"What colours do they come in?"

"Oh, there's fluorescent green and pink, black lycra and black leather with or without studs, sweetie. I highly recommend the studs." The woman gave an excited giggle.

"Green," Mel said firmly. "Is it okay if I pick

it up this afternoon?"

"Sure, sweetie," the woman purred. "We have plenty more in the Bang Him range that you might like."

Mel ended the call as quickly and politely as she could.

She and Lili drove to the adult shop and parked right out front, as Lili insisted, though it's not as if the shop had a back entrance or rear car park.

Inside the shop, they were greeted by an excited woman clad in black and silver latex. She couldn't stop expressing how thrilled she'd be to help them. Mel wondered whether this was the suspected product-tester she'd spoken to on the phone.

"We're here for the mankini? I rang earlier?" Mel asked hesitantly.

"Absolutely! Let me show you the whole range," the woman gushed. Her name badge read 'Mitzi'.

She took both girls over to a display that was clearly the province of the Bang Him range. Mel leaned over to look more closely at a strange-shaped item before she read the name and decided she didn't want to know what it did.

"Are you sure you want the green, sweetie?" Mitzi cooed, her hand waving toward a studded black vinyl number.

Mel choked as she spotted a dildo so big she wondered how anyone could use it for anything but decoration.

Lili answered, "Green would be lovely. It's for a work colleague."

"Oh, how delightful," Mitzi said with a wink. "Is there anything else you'd like?"

Mel tried to work out why they had a display of dildos with tentacles and what looked like strange torture implements, at 30% off, no less, in honour of the release of 'Monsters in the Dark', whatever they were, then decided that she didn't want to know that, either. Surely monsters should be kept in the dark, where they belonged…

"No, thank you," Mel managed to say, swallowing hard. She decided she'd rather be in Hell than here.

Eighteen

"Good morning, Gerry brought photos!" Lili told Mel as she arrived on Monday morning of another fresh week in HELL.

"Of what?" Mel asked, her mouth watering at the aroma of Lili's coffee.

Lili took a slow sip, savouring the taste with her eyes closed, before she swallowed and said, "Pictures his wife took of the mankini. He loved it – you're officially his favourite person in the office!"

Mel was ready to jump Lili for the coffee, she was panting for one. "Great." She forced herself to walk away.

Unlike Lili, Mel's budget didn't stretch to include expensive barista brew from the award-winning coffee shop downstairs, so she took her plain mug to the kitchen for some of the free instant stuff.

She grimaced as she took her first mouthful of watery, brown sludge, but the caffeine began to take effect, however crappy it tasted. She opened her email.

Gerry's big "THANK YOU!" email came with a slideshow. She clicked it open as she took another sip of her cup of almost-coffee — and almost spat it out on the monitor screen. By the time she was done with the slideshow, she knew that Gerry loved his mankini, it fitted him perfectly, he didn't have huge tufts of black hair poking out of it, and his wife really liked Gerry's reverse view, bisected by green lycra. Wait, were those her lips?

Mel decided that she sincerely hoped Gerry won the lottery that night. She wasn't sure she could look at him without thinking of his green mankini and arse-kissing wife.

Fighting to keep her coffee in her mouth,

she clicked on the next email at random, certain that it couldn't shock her more than the first. It was from a man she didn't know named Dan. It sounded like a nice, safe name.

She read it. She read it again, before deciding to find Lili. Surely it wasn't possible. This sounded like the story she'd been reading on the train.

Lili was riveted by something on her computer screen. Mel hoped it wasn't a disturbing PowerPoint presentation.

She cleared her throat. "Am I supposed to get conspiracy hoax emails?"

Lili looked up, annoyance clearly written across her face. "What?"

"Is there really an alien invasion?" Mel asked slowly, feeling silly.

"Aliens?" Lili looked blank for a moment. "Oh, yes, probably. You mean Dan's assessment that 'alien invaders don't hold back and if we're serious neither should we,' something about Yanks and 'collateral damage'?"

Mel nodded.

"Well, depending on what they'll affect, we'll

probably have to handle it in some capacity. Health, environment, life, lands…justice for whoever let them in…it all comes down to us."

Mel found her voice. "But, seriously…space aliens?"

Lili laughed. "If there are space aliens, we'd be the ones dealing with them. Dan's probably just talking about cane toads again."

"Oh." Mel sighed in relief.

"We'll have the Department of Defence to help with space aliens," Lili said. "For the terrestrial kind, we're on our own. Defence isn't any use against cane toads."

Nineteen

"Don't forget, software training today!" Lili called as Mel headed to the lunchroom in search of a hot drink. Mel nodded and kept walking. She just had time to get the tea and take it to the training room.

Slipping into a seat in the back row, she sipped her tea silently in the darkened room. A PowerPoint presentation lit the screen as well as a nervous Nybbas, who trembled at the front with a wobbling laser pointer in his hand. He looked more scared than she did, standing in front of an audience, Mel mused.

The trainer Mel recognised from her orientation, who she now knew was called Sil, shifted a tiny video camera on a tripod, angling it so it pointed right at Nybbas. "Right. As long as you stay between the tables and the screen, you're in the picture. We can send the training video out to all our regional offices as soon as this session's done."

Nybbas nodded, gnawing on his lip.

"And…you're live!" Sil sang out.

A sickly smile spread across Nybbas' face. "Good morning, er afternoon, er morning, ladies and gentlemen. Today I'm here to tell you how excited I am!" Between his gritted teeth and his stiff-armed pose, Mel's mind suggested several words that would be more appropriate than excited.

"This package will make you gasp in awe. Just one little thing that will change the way you work forever. I'm so excited to be giving it to you, I can barely contain myself. You're going to love it. And we'll be rolling it out across all the offices…"

The room full of bored demons transformed to one full of grinning demons, with enthusiasm far greater than anything Nybbas could show. His strained delivery of the rehearsed copy didn't help matters, either.

Mel pressed her lips together and endured Nybbas' presentation as best she could. He rushed through it so fast that he was done in only half their allotted time. Once the half-hour was up, a smiling Sil reached to turn off the video camera and the other demons congratulated Nybbas on his package, telling him how much the regional offices would enjoy the training session.

"I'll upload the video right away and send it out this afternoon," Sil said happily, cradling the camera.

"Wait."

Both Sil and Nybbas stared at Mel. Everyone else had left, but she still sat quietly in her seat.

"You should review the presentation first. Can we hook it up to the big screen, or only watch it from the recorder?" Mel asked.

"I guess I could upload it here..." Sil said. "I'll just go get the cables and stuff to hook it up. Be right back!"

She hurried out and Nybbas slumped onto a chair. "I was terrible, wasn't I? They were all lying when they said the regional offices would like my presentation…"

Mel took a careful breath. "No, not terrible. Look, if I gave you some suggestions as to how you might improve the presentation, maybe you'd like to record it again. Without an audience this time."

"Like what? I've had Sil coaching me for weeks on how to do a presentation. I have to use all the right words, move my hands, smile…I did all that!" Nybbas buried his face in his palms. "I can't do any better."

"Well, you know how you hold your hands sort of stiff at your sides," Mel began. She waited for Nybbas to nod before continuing, "You might want to consider lifting them a little. Instead of level with your hips, try making the same gesture in front of your chest, and widen your hands to about the width of your shoulders…"

"What do you mean?"

Mel tried to demonstrate. "You know how you hold your arms out like an Aussie Rules football umpire calling a goal? Your elbows bent close to your body, your forearms at right angles to the rest and your fingers pointing forward? Every time you gesture, it's so tight it looks like a pair of synchronised guillotines. If you lift your arms, your gestures are loose and seem more natural." She demonstrated the chopping motion Nybbas had used, then lifted her arms higher to show the difference.

Nybbas nodded slowly. "I could do that." He waved his arms experimentally, looking relieved.

"And keep your hands in front of your chest the whole time," Mel suggested, trying not to smile.

"I can do that, too," he replied. He stared at her. "But…I don't see why I should redo the whole presentation and record it again just to do the hand signals better. It seems such a tiny change. I'm sure the regional office staff won't notice the difference…"

Mel coughed delicately. "I think you'll find the small change in hand gestures will make a significant improvement to your overall delivery. I really do think it's worth it." Please don't make me say it any more plainly, Mel prayed.

Nybbas frowned at her and opened his mouth to protest.

"It's up!" Sil announced, striding into the room. Nybbas closed his mouth. "I uploaded it at my desk and it's on the network. I'll pull it up now…"

Mel closed her eyes and inhaled as she waited for the file to load. Sympathy for a devil was a terrible thing and she couldn't conscionably let Nybbas embarrass himself like this without attempting to intervene.

She bit down on her lip as the picture appeared. Nybbas' arms were held stiffly at his sides, his hands level with his pelvis, perhaps a sock's width apart. Every time his hands made a stiff guillotine chop, they neatly framed his open pants fly. The slight pull on his pants fabric made the unbuttoned gap in the front of his boxers pop open, revealing a tantalising glimpse of flesh.

"…ladies and (chop) gentlemen. Today (chop) I'm here (chop) to tell (chop) you how excited (chop) I am!" It was very clear from the lack of bulging that he was either not the slightest bit excited, or his excitement was contained within a very small space.

Mel forced herself to continue watching, if only for Nybbas' benefit. She didn't dare laugh.

"This (chop) package (chop) will make you gasp (chop chop) in awe…"

The demon on the screen placed his thumb and forefinger a finger's width apart and shook them at pelvis level for emphasis, before returning to chopping.

"Just (shake) one (shake) little (shake) thing (shake) that will change (chop) the way you work forever (chop). I'm (chop) so (chop chop) excited to be giving it to you, I can barely contain (chop) myself. You're going to love (chop) it. And we'll be rolling it out across all the offices…"

Mercifully, Mel reached over and paused the video.

"Holy Hell. I can't believe no one told me. I almost showed my dick to the whole corporation…" Nybbas' eyes looked wider than the distance between his shaking fingers in the presentation.

"And told them it was only an inch long!" Sil burst out, laughing.

Mel kept her voice level. "Sil, could you go get that camera? I'll help Nybbas record a more appropriate training package." She kept her eyes on Sil until the trainer hurried out of the room, mumbling her assent.

"I'll be in your debt forever for this, Mel," Nybbas vowed. "Eternally grateful…anything you need, you just ask. And if you help me do the presentation again without telling everyone about my tiny package, I'll be your personal slave for life."

Smiling uncertainly, Mel waved away the offer. "It's really not necessary. I just like to help."

Nybbas' eyes grew round. "Is it because you think I'm tiny? Honestly, I'm not. I may not be as big as Lord Lucifer, but it's not small and I definitely know how to use it. I helped build the Thai adult film industry, I'll have you know. Here, let me show you…" He unbuttoned his pants and dropped them to his ankles.

Now Mel laughed – albeit gently. "It's okay

– I believe you. I really don't need to see it. Put your pants back on – you'll need them to do your presentation. And make sure that zip's secure…" Mel averted her eyes as he complied. Over her shoulder, she continued, "Would you like to do it right away, or would you prefer to do your presentation some other time?"

"I have to send it out as soon as possible, so I'd better do it now. With HR booking the room every day to work on their group Christmas presentation, I'll never get this meeting room again," Nybbas replied, sighing. "OH! Right after I feed the imps. The last time I was late feeding them, we had horny demons all over the place. Would you like to meet them?"

"Ah…horny demons? No, thank you, I think I've met more than my fair share already and…"

Nybbas laughed. "I mean the imps. Didn't you ever wonder how we manage to hide our existence from humans and blend in so well?"

"Yes," Mel admitted. "Sure. I'd love to meet your imps."

Twenty

"Come with me. I'll show you where we get their food," Nybbas said, striding out of the training room. He held the door to Reception open for Mel and she thanked him. "Have to go downstairs." He punched the button for the lift, which opened precisely three seconds later. Both he and Mel entered and travelled to the ground floor, before Mel followed him into the shopping arcade beside the HELL Corporation building.

"Their favourite is the peri-peri chips from Nando's in the food court," Nybbas explained.

"I get two seriously large serves with extra chili salt once a week. Other days, they get the spiciest Thai I can find. I'll let you give them the chips – they'll love you for it. They don't normally take too well to new people, so their favourite food will help…"

He helped himself to the chips on their lift ride back to the office, before leading the way to IT and the server room. At the door, he passed the chips to Mel and fished through his pockets. Nybbas withdrew a key with his peri-powdered fingers and poked it into the server room door. "They live in here. It has better climate control than the rest of the office." He opened the door and frigid air froze Mel's fingers. "Come on in."

Mel carefully stepped inside the server room, which had a wall occupied by blinking racks of equipment that looked like the office's computer servers. Blue umbilical network cables connected them through the ceiling to the whole corporation, and hanging from the cables were what looked like black bats.

"Chip day, boys," Nybbas called, letting the door close behind them. Wings unfolded and leathery faces peered out, but none relinquished their grip on the cables. "Hold up the bags," he murmured to Mel.

She did, but their response didn't change. Mel set the bags on the small, empty table in the middle of the room and ripped one bag down the front. The spicy smell of the salt wafted up, tempting even her.

Claws ticked on the laminate as a bat landed beside her hand. The creature regarded Mel with soul-searching eyes that belonged to no bat she'd ever met. She smiled in response. It extended a claw toward her and she took it in her fingers.

"Respect, lady," she heard the creature say, though its mouth never moved.

"Thank you," her spirit replied, equally silently. She glanced at Nybbas. "Can the demon hear us?"

"Demons poor soul-readers. Not like you, lady. For illusion-weaver, soul-talk is simple."

"Illusion-weaver?"

The creature showed her images of his people. "Unweave illusions for you, lady. Sptlk show?"

Mel understood that the string of consonants was the imp's name. "Sure."

Sptlk gazed deeply into Mel's eyes and she could feel the imp's soul touch hers. "Lady now can see illusion or reality. Respect, lady. See demon or batman." Mel followed the imp's glance to where Nybbas had stood only minutes before, but he appeared to have vanished. In his place stood a demon so dark he blended into the racks behind him, only visible because he blocked the blinking lights. With his pointed horns and wings, he did look cartoonish. Batman, indeed.

She turned startled eyes on the imps above Nybbas' head. Instead of bats, they looked more like small, round, winged demons, in varying shades of red and black. Sptlk himself was deep burgundy and he sported a pot belly. He patted it happily. "Many chip days."

Mel laughed and the sound was loud in the enclosed space. She blinked carefully and the imps were bats once more. Another blink and she saw Sptlk's very human fingers reach for a chip. He saluted her with it. "Thanks, lady." Sharp teeth demolished chip and chili salt quickly.

"Just like you like 'em, right, Spike?" Nybbas asked, grinning at the imp.

Sptlk nodded and the other imps seemed to decide this was their cue to celebrate chip day, too.

"So these are imps? And they keep you hidden…how?" Mel asked carefully.

Nybbas shrugged. "No idea how they do it. They weave some sort of illusion that people can't penetrate – it even works on us. Hell, they even do it in Hell. Lord Lucifer said they were living in Hell when he got there and they agreed to help him run the place. No idea what he offered them in return."

Sptlk winked at Mel. "Illusion for illusion. Illusion-weavers build illusions for Hell. Illusion-weavers holiday here with humans. Illusion of intimacy and privacy. Much comedy. Lord of Hell very seductive man. Or woman."

Luce in a skirt. No, Luce in stockings and a corset. Seducing how many while the imps watched and laughed? Mel managed a smile. "I'm sure he is," she replied silently.

"Soul-reader who can see through illusions sees deep truth beneath lies. Respect, lady, and hope."

"Thank you," she said, hoping the imp could sense the depth of her gratitude.

The imp nodded sagely in response.

"Wow – they sure like you. I've never seen Spike acknowledge anyone else who's come into the server room. You're not like anyone I've ever met, Mel." Nybbas blushed.

"Maybe you don't meet many angels," Mel suggested.

He shook his head. "No, I've met a fair few angels. None like you, though. You're definitely different. Hell, I don't know any angel who'd have helped me with my presentation. We should probably leave these boys to it and do that video. I'm so happy it'll be just you watching this time, Mel."

Mel saw Sptlk hide a grin. "Demons fun to watch." She smothered her own laugh as she followed Nybbas back to the training room so he could present his package. Hopefully, with his fly zipped up this time.

Twenty-one

"Mel, come to lunch with us," Merih said, glancing at Gerry and Lili. There were a fair few other people grouped behind them, too, all carrying sunglasses.

"Hmm? Oh, no, I brought a sandwich," Mel said.

"You can't sit in the office and just eat a home-made sandwich on Melbourne Cup Day. You have to go out to lunch. If we have to drag you out kicking and screaming, you're coming," Merih insisted. He grabbed her wrist.

Mel felt the jolt of energy that flung Merih

back against the wall. It probably hurt her as much as it had him, but he'd taken the full force of it so she barely moved. "Are you okay?" she asked, concerned.

Merih rubbed his arm as the others backed away, murmuring about how they'd meet him there.

"No wonder angels never see any action. Can't even touch them without getting burned," someone muttered.

"I'm sorry," Mel said. "That's never happened before." She stared at her hand, touching her fingers to the desk to see if there was any further discharge. No, not even the slightest spark of static.

"Well, if there was ever any uncertainty about you being an angel, that's gone now," Merih said with a weak grin. "Damn, I forgot about that. It's been ages since I tried to touch an angel and almost never since I started working in the Pit. Didn't you know angels burn demons on contact? Something about the difference in souls — negative and positive energy annihilating each other. Ah, the engineers in Infrastructure can explain it better than me."

Mel frowned. "But I shook hands with Lili when I first started here and she didn't get hurt. And I'm sure I've bumped into or brushed against people here and not hurt anyone..."

"That's different." Merih shrugged. "Angels can control it – shield themselves, somehow, if they want to. Demons can't. Or maybe it's something about intent – an accidental touch doesn't set it off unless there's intent to harm. It's not body contact so much as souls touching. It also means none of us can jump you in the photocopy room without your consent." He sighed.

Mel laughed. "No one's tried that yet." Except Luce and his attempts at issuing orders, she thought, but that wasn't the same as using force. For all his arrogance, he hadn't attempted to touch her. Perhaps she was safer here than Raphael had thought.

Merih's voice brought her thoughts out of Luce's office and back to her own cramped cubicle. "It's still hard to believe you're an angel, though, even after..." He flexed his hand, wincing.

It had to be the first time anyone had ever doubted she was an angel. "Why?"

"Well, you talk to us," Merih admitted. "Treat us like people, like you're one of us and not one of them."

Mel tried not to laugh, but she couldn't keep the gentle smile off her face. "What do you expect me to do? Wander around pretending you don't exist? I know there are differences between angels and demons, and now that I know I can hurt you if I touch you I'll try to be more careful, but I can't see why I'd want to ignore you. Why would other angels do that?"

"I haven't had much luck getting answers out of them," Merih said. "But from what they say to each other, they're afraid they'll be tainted by contact with us. Even just a word or a glance. Like I'd want to touch some snotty, stuck-up angel who'd probably scream and faint the first time she saw a pair of hairy balls and a stiff prick..." He coughed. "Sorry."

This time Mel did laugh. "I can't recall ever fainting at such a sight. Screaming, perhaps, but that came later..." She glanced up at

Merih, registering his shock. "What? Haven't you seen an angel blush before?"

Merih swallowed and licked his lips, looking like there were a few things he wanted to say, but didn't dare. "You've got to be the most unusual angel I've ever met." He eyed her hands warily. "If I can't drag you, I guess I'll have to appeal to your sense of charity."

Mel stared at him. Demons didn't support charity.

"You know how wonderful the coffee here is?" he began. Mel smiled and nodded. "Alright, we actually have better coffee in Hell. The instant stuff here is part of some government contract that doesn't expire for another three years, so we can't get out of it. But the German Beer Café up the road is hosting a huge Melbourne Cup lunch and we've all bought tickets. There are all sorts of giveaways, including a brand-new coffee machine — one that uses those little capsule things. We figure that the more of us who go, the better our chance of winning one and we'll pay whoever wins a share of what the machine is worth to use it, so we aren't drinking shit any more."

"Then good luck. I hope you get it," Mel replied. She turned her eyes back to her computer screen.

"We won't unless you come," he said bluntly. "We only go into the draw if our table has at least ten people and we're nine without you."

Mel sighed. "So I have to come to save you from bad coffee?" Her fingers skipped across the keyboard, locking access to her computer. Swinging her access pass lanyard down from the shelf, Mel said, "There's a story in the making – an angel saving a demon. If it were more interesting, maybe someone might write a book about it one day. Ah, the coffee would have to be pretty foul to be worth sticking in a story."

Grabbing her mug, she downed the dregs of cold coffee, almost choking as the sludge hit her tongue. "Honestly, I think this stuff could have come from the sewers in Hell. Not even the damned deserve to drink this. Let's go."

Twenty-two

"Great! You brought her. Now we're ten and we're going to win that coffee machine." Gerry waved the hostess over. "Table for ten from HELL Corporation, please." He turned to Mel and Merih. "We've all ordered. Tell the girl at the counter what you want and don't forget to enter the sweep!"

The others trooped off in the hostess' wake as Merih stepped up to the register. "I'll have a jug of the darkest house beer you have and…how does the food work?"

The harassed-looking woman at the register

eyed the queue behind them. "If you're on a company table, then it's twenty dollars a head for food, and drinks are extra," she said. "How many horses do you want in the sweep? Just one?"

"Sounds good to me," Merih replied, handing over his credit card.

The woman processed his payment and held out a basket full of folded paper slips. "Pick your horse," she said.

Merih dipped his hand into the basket, his nails scraping against the bottom, and pulled out a slip. "Red Cadeaux!" he announced, then frowned. "Never heard of it."

"And you, miss?" the woman asked, looking expectantly at Mel.

"Oh, just a glass of your lightest wheat beer — the Weihenstephaner, please. I'm on the same corporate table and…I need a horse, right?"

"You don't have to," Merih jumped in, looking worried. "It's not like you need to gamble if you don't want to."

"You can't enjoy the Melbourne Cup properly without one," the woman said, giving

Merih a dirty look. "It's dull if you're not screaming for your horse for that last lap of the race."

Mel laughed. "I'll take the lunch, the beer and the horse, please. I wouldn't want to miss an opportunity to do a bit of screaming." Out of the corner of her eye, she saw Merih blush as red as the Beck's shield on the wall behind him. She handed over her money.

"I hope you pick a winner, then," the woman said, offering the basket.

Mel shrugged. "Green Moon will win, but it's about enjoying the race, so I'll take…" She selected a slip. "…Lights of Heaven. That's a well-named horse for me."

"You never know. It's the Melbourne Cup. Any horse could win," the woman said.

Mel just smiled and followed Merih to the crowded table where their colleagues sat, already munching on the first round of garlic bread.

The two remaining free places at the table were right beside the window. One of the chairs was bathed in the bright, near-noon sun. Merih sat in the shaded one as Mel reached for the other, only to recoil the moment her fingers touched it: the surface of the metal chair was hot enough to fry her lunch on.

Someone sniggered, but Mel heard Merih say, "We should ask for another chair. Mel shouldn't have to…"

"I'll be fine," Mel cut in. She nudged the chair away from the table with her foot, careful to only touch the scorching metal with her shoe. She reached for the jug of iced water and poured it carefully over the chair, making sure she didn't wet her colleagues. Steam rose and a few chunks of ice clattered to the concrete floor, but she didn't flinch until the jug was empty. She reached for the other jug and did the same. Nine demons watched in silence as the puddle on the floor started to evaporate.

Reaching for the last slice of garlic bread, she whipped the cloth out of the basket beneath and used it to dry her much-cooled chair. Crunching into the crust, she smiled as she sat down. A wide-eyed waiter behind her set her beer on the table with shaking hands and she thanked him. He took the empty jugs from her and promised to refill them.

A platter of tempura prawns arrived at the table, followed by another with a tepee of prosciutto-wrapped asparagus spears, and the distracted demons decided it was safe to start talking again.

Mel ate without speaking, occasionally sipping her beer, as she listened to Lili and the girl beside her discussing some book they'd been reading. It seemed to involve some particularly violent sex and a man called Quincy.

She couldn't help herself. "I'm sorry…a violent, sadistic villain called Quincy? With a name like that, I imagine he has a fair bit to be angry about."

"Have you read the Monsters in the Dark series?" Lili asked, surprised.

"No," Mel admitted. "It sounds a bit dark for me, to be honest."

Lili turned away to talk to the man on her other side.

"So you're the angel," the girl beside Mel said. "I never thought I'd see one of your kind at a Melbourne Cup lunch. I mean — isn't gambling a sin to you? Like drinking…and generally enjoying yourself? Or even talking to the likes of us?"

Mel smiled gently. "The rest of the office were going – it seemed rude not to. And Merih told me you needed the numbers to have a chance at better coffee in the office. I wanted to help. I'm perfectly happy to drink and enjoy myself. I even have a horse in the sweep." She held up the little slip of paper.

"Then you're already halfway to being one of the CEO's little office whores. I swear he has a collection of temps just like you that he's corrupted so quickly you'd think they'd never seen a man before. Has he broken you in over his desk yet?" The girl gave a knowing grin at Mel's shock. "What, did you think you were the first?"

"Ana, leave Mel alone," Merih interjected. "If Luce finds out you've been spreading rumours, it'll be you over that desk and you know it."

Ana gave a disgusted sniff and lurched to her feet, headed for the counter and what Mel suspected would be another drink.

"Don't listen to her, Mel," Merih continued.

"Luce does have a reputation for seducing all the new office temps – human and angel – but you're different to them. Just don't accept any meetings alone in his office with him and you should be fine." He became very interested in the plate of spring rolls that appeared in front of him as Lili glared in his direction across Ana's empty seat.

"It's all right," Mel said softly as Ana returned, bearing a jug of beer and a glass that she thumped down on the table. "He's already made an attempt."

"Ah Hell, Mel, I didn't realise. I'm sorry…"

Mel shrugged. "I turned him down. I also suggested he might want to clean his desk occasionally, given all the action it's seen."

Merih exploded in laughter, spraying beer across the table. It missed Mel but splattered in Lili's face, sending her eyeliner running. Lili jumped to her feet, beer and murder in her eyes.

"I believe I'll get another drink. Would anyone else like one?" Mel asked the table in general.

The others got up to dig through their

pockets for cash, neatly boxing Lili in at her seat and out of reach of Merih. Mel heard his muttered thanks before she headed up to the counter, trying to remember everyone's beer preferences. She decided to stick to water. Let the demons get drunk – she had work to do when she returned to the office.

Twenty-three

The whole café fell silent. Mel couldn't hear the crunch of a single chip.

"Aaaand…they're off!" the race caller shouted.

Twenty-four horses jumped from their starting stalls on the large-screen TVs, their thundering hooves the only sound inside the café.

The race caller identified the horses and their relative positions as the animals galloped their riders round the first lap of Flemington Racecourse.

That's when the shouting started, rising in a crescendo as the jockeys whipped their horses down the final straight. It wasn't just the demons, either – every single human in the café seemed to be shrieking their support for their respective horse, though the beasts on the other side of the country certainly couldn't hear them.

Mel watched with satisfaction as Green Moon did, indeed, cross the finish line first, followed by three horses with odd names that were much harder to remember. None of these horses were on her or Merih's slips.

Or any other demon's, oddly enough. The demons flung their slips on the table, with varying combinations of anger, disappointment and disgust. She wondered why they bothered gambling at all – after all, demons' bad luck was legendary.

The sweep winners approached the counter to claim their prizes. One was a man who'd had to reject a promotion because his wife had recently given birth to twins and suffered from crippling postnatal depression. Another was a girl who sent all her spare money home to her family in Indonesia, in the hope that her little sister could come and visit sometime soon. The third winner seemed to live a charmed life, but her boss had excused himself early to finalise the paperwork to make her position redundant – a fate she wasn't yet aware of, but she would be by the end of the day. Mel sighed – such was the way of the world, especially in times like these.

The hostess at the counter picked up a handbell and rang it, sending the café silent again. "We'll be drawing the raffle prizes, too. Last chance to buy a ticket – the proceeds go to the winter blanket appeal for the city's homeless." She gestured at the waitstaff who were waving ticket books.

Mel jumped to her feet. "One for me, please." Nine demons stared at her as a waiter wove through the tables to take her money. It wasn't that she wanted or needed any of the raffle prizes, whatever those might be. She couldn't refuse charity – nor a request for help – and this was both. She ignored the demonic scrutiny as she traded her money for a ticket. Number 888, apparently.

The hostess cleared her throat. "Now, everyone on one of the corporate tables, I'm going to ask you to check beneath you. Taped to the bottom of your chair are your free tickets into the draw."

Mel realised that none of the demons had bought a ticket – all they had were the free ones that were included as part of their meal. No, demons definitely didn't believe in charity.

She reached under her seat for hers and almost laughed when she saw the ticket number. Someone sure had a sense of humour up there.

The first half-dozen prizes were coffee, beer and meal vouchers, which went to various human patrons.

"Next up are two coffee pod machines," the hostess announced, as a grinning waiter carried them forward like he was the proud father of twins. She drew out the first ticket. "Four five seven!"

Mel and the increasingly irritated demons watched as first one, then the other coffee maker were won by humans. It definitely wasn't the demons' day. Not only were they damned, but they were doomed to drink disgusting coffee while they were on Earth.

"And one last prize that only came in yesterday. When our coffee supplier heard what we were giving away, he said he'd provide another prize for one lucky winner who appreciated real coffee. So we'll draw one more ticket for an office coffee maker – the same model we use here – and the first year's supply of coffee beans, all provided by our sales rep." The hostess coughed. "For those of you who don't win, we have some brochures for you to take back to your office, detailing prices and packages for machines and coffee supply…"

The demons perked up considerably at this. One of them muttered in Latin, the words too fast for Mel to make out.

"The winning ticket is…number six six six!"

Someone laughed.

Mel's colleagues looked feverishly through the tickets on the table. Gerry lifted the salt shaker, muttering, "Has to be one of us. It has to be…" – looking for a missing ticket that definitely wasn't there.

"Redraw!" a man seated near the door

bellowed. The cry was taken up by several others.

Someone definitely had a strange sense of humour, Mel decided. But not even demons deserved to drink the sewage sludge back at the office and she'd be damned before she'd deny them some hope in their miserable lives. She rose. "It's mine." Holding up the ticket that had been taped to the underside of her Hell-hot chair, the angel calmly made her way to the hostess and handed it over.

"Where do you work?" the hostess asked. "I need the office address for the supplier, as he'll deliver your fresh coffee beans weekly – I only have a week's worth here to go with the machine." She gestured at the huge box that was definitely more than Mel could carry.

"I work for the HELL Corporation," Mel replied, writing down the address.

The hostess snorted. "You'll need all the perks you can get, working in that Hell-hole. I've heard stories…well, at least you'll have decent coffee for when you're forced to work late. I've heard it happens a lot over there."

"Not to me," Mel said cheerfully. "Thank

you, though. I think my colleagues will appreciate it when the shock wears off." It was hard to ignore nine demons staring at you, she mused.

"Get a couple of the blokes to help you carry it, then, and another couple to grab the coffee. There's a lot and it's heavy," the woman cautioned.

Mel smiled, nodded and thanked her again, before returning to the table.

Merih clapped hard. "Way to go, Mel!"

Slowly, the others joined in with half-hearted applause.

"I can't carry it back to the office myself," she admitted. "Would some of you be willing to help?"

She was answered by demonic silence.

Mel shrugged. "I guess I could ask if the staff here have a trolley I could borrow. I don't think it'll fit in the kitchen, though. Do you think we might be able to set it up on a table in the lunchroom?"

"You mean you're bringing that thing to our office and not the agency?" Lili blurted out.

Mel laughed. "Of course. I work in your

office, not the agency office. I'd say your need is greater, too, and you all did invite me along today…"

Two demons whose names Mel didn't know stood up and marched to the counter. Between them, they lifted the coffee machine. "Are you ready to go?" one asked her.

Mel nodded. "There's the coffee, too…"

Merih swung one big bag of coffee beans into Gerry's arms and hefted the other in his own. "At your service, Mel. We'll have to work out how much we owe you for this."

Mel waved the offer away. "I can't drink all this coffee on my own and it'd be a shame not to share it. You don't need to."

"I'll arrange it with everyone else in the office. We'll call it the coffee club. We'd pay one of our own and just because you're not a demon, doesn't mean you don't deserve…"

One of the machine-toting demons cut in: "Oi, this is heavy, mate. If you're going to stand around and talk, you can carry the coffee machine."

"Right. Right," Merih replied, as he led the procession back to the sixth floor of the

HELL Corporation building.

Twenty-four

In front of an audience of what seemed like half the office, Mel broke the coffee machine out of the box and attempted to assemble it. It was easier than she'd expected, but the LCD screen wasn't lighting up. It took ten minutes before she realised that no one had plugged it in yet and the dearth of helpful volunteers seemed to be standard procedure in HELL.

"There's a power point under this table. Here, I'll hook it up and we can try that again," Mel said, dropping to her knees to crawl under the furniture. Mel heard the scrape of shoes on carpet and wondered why the demons behind her were moving around. She was wearing pants today, so she knew they weren't jockeying for a better view of her underwear.

"So who do I have to whip to get some work done around here?" Mel heard Luce's voice.

She couldn't reach the socket yet. It was half-hidden under a cabinet beside the table. Scooting along the carpet, her fingers made contact with the dusty power point and she plugged the machine in.

"You won the coffee machine at the Cup lunch? It's about time we had some decent coffee around here. Hell, for that, you can all have the afternoon off."

Nobody moved except Mel, whose fingers scrabbled for the switch to turn the power on. There was so much dust behind the cabinet — or were those cobwebs? It looked like Luce's desk wasn't the only thing in the office that the cleaning staff didn't have time for.

"Who won it, anyway? I'll offer a blowjob to the man, if he makes me the first coffee with that thing."

Stunned silence as Mel covered her mouth with a dusty hand to stop herself from exploding into laughter. She decided to get out from under the table before things got out of hand. No one would believe Luce had offered his employees…much less her…

Mel emerged from under the table, but the demons in the room screened her from Luce's sight, even as she stood up.

"Not from me, personally, of course. You can have your pick of the office girls. The new one's pretty and has quite a clever mouth on her, too. In fact, I can vouch for her myself."

She couldn't help it any more. Luce was digging a hole so deep, he'd hit Hell soon if she didn't stop him. Her laughter bubbled up and out, breaking the demonic silence. "That would be me."

Demons shuffled aside, letting Mel see Luce's surprised expression. He recovered quickly. "Perfect timing. Now, who's going to turn down this lovely lady's services? All you have to do is make me a coffee…"

Mel cleared her throat. "Actually, I don't know how." She glanced around, wondering who had the manual for the machine.

Luce laughed. "Nothing to it! Just drop to your knees, open your mouth, relax your throat and drink down what comes."

Twenty-five

"I think there's a bit more to making a coffee on this machine. Merih, can you please pass me the manual? I'll need a cup, too." Mel accepted the booklet and one of the dozen proffered cups with a smile of thanks. "How do you take your coffee, Luce? Or should I guess? I would say…an espresso. Or a double, given the size of the cup. Just the bitter brew, with no milk, cream or sugar."

Luce's smile was as tight and uncomfortable as a brand-new pair of jeans that was a size too small, but his tone still sounded confident.

"That sounds about right."

Mel glanced at the manual, keying in his selection. The coffee machine whirred as it started making his brew. Mel kept her eyes carefully on the filling cup as she heard the shuffle of moving feet behind her once more. She spun on the spot with the hot drink in her hands, holding it out to Luce. "The first cup. Enjoy." Her smile was sincere.

He took it from her and slurped at the contents. The demons who hadn't already made their escape decided as one that this was the best time to do so.

Mel held her ground, not lowering her lips from their smile. She didn't laugh when she saw the scrawled text on the side of the mug serendipity had bestowed on Luce – 'SEXY DEVIL', it said. Sad, frustrated, soon to be embarrassed devil would have been more appropriate, but pity stayed her tongue from saying so. Instead, she said, "How's the coffee? I've never used such a complicated machine before. I'm hoping someone who has more experience can show me how to use it."

Luce carefully set his cup down. He glanced

around, checking to make sure they really were alone before he spoke in a very low voice. "You're the one who won the coffee machine, aren't you?" Mel nodded once. "Why did you bring it here, instead of the agency where you work? Angels always look after angels first." He sounded bitter.

Mel kept her voice gentle. "Actually, we don't. We look after those who need it most. Those who have the least. I've never worked for Raphael in that office – just here. This office is a pretty dark place and I thought it could do with a bit of hope. No one deserved to drink the coffee we had here before – damned or not, it was just plain horrible." She managed an apologetic smile. "Besides, angels aren't addicted to caffeine like your staff are. We can easily do without. If your staff weren't so afraid of you, perhaps one of them might have said something before you made an offer you couldn't deliver on."

Luce grinned. "Sure I can. Your pick of the office girls – or anyone else here. The technique might be a little different to a blowjob, but I'm sure they'd do their bit to thank you. After all, I'm always open to a more permanent arrangement with our temporary staff, if you like it here."

Mel shook her head, remembering Raphael's warning. "No, Luce. I'm not getting intimate with any of your staff, nor do I want a permanent job here."

"What about me?" His grin faltered, but it was still there. "I'm quite a sexy devil, you know, and I do have a fair bit of experience." His eyes didn't seem so cold now – the darkness reminded her more of his steaming cup of coffee than the vacuum of space. "I'm only offering this to you, Mel. How about a hot cup of sensuality in payment for this equally hot cup of coffee?"

This took her by surprise. Oral sex from Lucifer himself – well, there was an offer a girl didn't get every day, much less an angel. He'd even remembered her name. "Luce, all I really wanted was a decent cup of coffee for myself. Giving the same to everyone else in the office is a perk, I guess."

Luce looked thoughtful. "How about I make you one? My coffee machine at home is just a smaller version of this one. I should be able to work it out. How do you take it?"

Mel shrugged. "I usually drink tea. I occasionally have a cup of instant coffee, but not often enough to be able to say I know what I like. I'm sure whatever you make will be fine."

"A macchiato, but I'll make it a double because you have a mug…and top it up. White and fluffy on top, clothed in light brown, just like the suit you wore to your interview, but with a hidden dark heart inside." Luce looked proud of himself.

"It sounds lovely, Luce, but you're wrong about a macchiato – or at least, how it's supposed to be made. The heart of a macchiato is milk-white," Mel said gently. She'd never seen such a clumsy attempt at corrupting her – so much for the seductive devil she'd been warned about. All she felt was sympathy for this devil, not desire at all.

His eyes seemed to darken. "We'll see." He stabbed the buttons on the coffee machine until it whirred in submission. Both he and Mel watched the spout, from the first dark trickle to the last white droplet. "Hmmph. Maybe you're right," he said grudgingly.

Mel reached for her cup and took a tiny sip. She licked the foam from her lip and smiled. "I usually am, but you made a good call on this coffee. I like it. Thank you."

Luce just stared at her, as if he didn't believe her, or he suspected some ulterior motive behind her taste for his coffee-making skills. Mel sighed and waited. She didn't know how demons managed to live with this sort of distrust.

She took pity on him. "I'm an angel, remember? Angels don't lie, Luce."

It took a moment, but eventually Luce seemed satisfied and he relaxed. "No worries," he said. "You're not like any other angel I've known – and I've known a fair few."

Mel smiled. "So I've been told."

Luce seemed to hesitate, torn between more than one course of action. Mel hoped he didn't do anything else stupid.

He seized her hand and kissed it.

Mel expected another jolt of electricity to throw him across the room, like it had with

Merih that morning. Some pain as two opposing souls touched. Or some sort of tingling, core-wrenching reaction that so frequently happened to the heroines in all the human romances she'd read. Yet she felt nothing – just the damp touch of his lips on the back of her hand and a faint impression of stormy clouds. That's all she caught of his soul before he released her.

Where was the darkness she'd seen before? Mel wondered. Storm clouds were nowhere near as dark, nor as thick. Was the absence of darkness an illusion…or the darkness itself? She blinked, twice, but Luce didn't change. Unlike Nybbas, Luce looked the same with or without illusion. No, wait, there was one place he'd want to look more impressive. Staring hard at the front of Luce's pants, Mel tried to work out which bulge was the illusion and which the reality, but they both looked identical.

Luce cleared his throat. Startled, Mel looked up. "If you're feeling the same way, I'd be happy to help."

Mel stared. She felt relieved that she hadn't

hurt him. One demon a day was more than enough.

"My offer still stands," Luce continued with a wink.

"Your offer?"

"Of very personal payment for your first coffee," Luce replied, raising the cup in salute. "Any time." Whistling, he wandered off.

Mel almost wiped her damp hand on her pants, but she waited until he was out of sight before crossing to the kitchen, where she washed her hands instead. Who knew where his mouth had been?

Twenty-Six

"Enjoy your holiday!" Gerry called, grinning, as Mel left for the day. "Don't forget to bring back photos!"

"I'll do my best," she replied, shouldering her way through the door to Reception. If she did bring pictures, she'd make sure there wasn't a single mankini in any of them.

Mel's phone rang before she'd pushed her way through the supposedly automatic doors in the lobby. She glanced at the number before accepting the call. "Hi, Raphael."

"Mel, it's me, Raphael," he said, as if he

hadn't heard her. Mel waited patiently for his mind to catch up with his mouth. "I've got Gabi! She's arrived from Russia and she'll be in first thing tomorrow to start her receptionist job at HELL. You won't be alone any more!"

"I leave for Sri Lanka tonight and I won't be back for over a week, Raphael. She'll just have to settle in without me."

"You're going WHERE?"

Mel took a deep breath. "I'm going to Sri Lanka. I've had this planned for months, since well before you asked me to go to the job interview here in HELL. Flights and accommodation booked, the works. I'm not giving up my trip to Colombo for you or this job."

"But why are you going to Sri Lanka? Why now? Can't it wait? How can a holiday be more important than stopping Lucifer from taking over the world?" Raphael wailed.

"Raphael, CHOGM is in Colombo this year. I haven't missed a single meeting and not even Lucifer himself will stop me from attending this one. I have a life outside of the agency and the HELL Corporation, remember? You can keep me from Korea for a bit, but not Sri Lanka. Do you have any idea how much trouble world leaders can cause in a retreat without an angel? You remember the one in New Zealand, back in '95?"

Silence reigned as Raphael remembered, all too well, his failings of that year. "You know I'm sorry about that, Mel. It should have been you in Nigeria, not me, but by the time I realised, it was too late. I…Have a good trip and try to enjoy yourself. Get some rest. Something tells me you'll need it."

Mel once again promised she'd do her best, before ending the call. Slipping her phone back into her bag, she marched off to the train station, mentally listing all the things she needed to pack. She knew it was quite hot in Colombo this time of year. Hell, it was hot in Colombo every day of the year. Thank God her hotel had a pool.

Twenty-Seven

Mel rose from the water, refreshed by her morning swim. With the conference dinner last night, the festivities had ended and she had until the following evening to rest, recuperate and reconcile herself to returning home to her job at the HELL Corporation. Lucifer and his minions be damned. Why couldn't she go back to living the life she was supposed to?

"Don't you just look like the angel of the morning, rising from the foam like Venus," a male voice remarked.

Mel's eyes darted to the reclining man.

"Watch your words. Lucifer was the light of the morning, and if that's me, you're in for one Hell of a seduction – that will end with you losing your soul."

"But you're not," he said, sliding his sunglasses from his face. "You're the Melody Angel. An angel far more seductive than that old devil could ever be. I knew there was another angel here, but it wasn't until I saw you in the pool this morning that I knew for sure. I should've known. So much harmony at one of these meetings – so many world leaders singing the same tune…must've been visited by the Melody Angel. And who else would be brave enough to swim in a white bikini?" He lifted his camera. "May I?"

"Sure," Mel replied, flashing a perfunctory smile as the camera clicked. She waited for him to lower the camera before throwing her body into the sun lounge beside his. Mel closed her eyes and heard more clicks. "Patrick, if you don't put the camera down, I'm going to throw it in the pool. Just like the last one, when we were in Perth."

"Good thing it's waterproof, then. I'm

learning. What can I get you to drink?"

Mel squinted at him. "This early in the morning? Coffee and juice, which I'm going to drink in reverse order."

"Yes, madam," a hotel waiter murmured. Mel hadn't seen him until he'd spoken. She thanked him quickly.

"Better get me a big coffee, too," Patrick said. The sunglasses covered his eyes again. "How come you look so fresh after last night's banquet? Didn't you drink at all?"

"Sure I did. A few glasses of wine over the course of the evening. I didn't see you there, though. I bet you finished off all of their best Scotch." Mel shook her head. "You and your whisky…"

"Ah, it's because the weather's too hot here for my kilt," Patrick responded. "If I'd been wearing that, you wouldn't have had eyes for anyone else, I bet."

Mel laughed. "You have me there. You in a kilt and nothing else is a temptation for any girl, angel or not. And I know what you keep under it."

"If I'd known you'd be here, I would have

packed it anyway, Mel, and to Hell with the weather," Patrick said. "What do you have planned for the day? Or do you fly out today?"

"Tomorrow night, I fly out," Mel replied. "Today and tomorrow, I'd planned on just exploring a bit of Sri Lanka. Being a tourist for a tiny bit before I go home and…aah, Raphael's got this crazy idea that Lucifer's loose in Western Australia and laying the foundations for a new takeover bid. I'm helping him find out what's really going on."

"Lucifer? Well, that doesn't surprise me. Aren't the caves of Hell in the West Australian desert? He had to move them a while back due to overcrowding and there's plenty of space to expand there, if you don't mind the killer wildlife. Of course he'd start there – it's close to home for him." Patrick sat up. "Spend the day with me, Mel. Tomorrow, too, if you like. I have a boat booked with some friends. Come join me for a bit of wahoo. I know you'll like it." He winked.

Mel looked at Patrick. Even in shorts and an open shirt, he looked sexy as Hell. She didn't do demons, but angels were a different story –

especially one she knew as well as Patrick. She waited while the waiter set out their drinks, thanking the man and handing him a tip before he disappeared. Sipping her juice, she replied, "First, explain to me exactly what you plan in terms of wahoo."

Twenty-eight

"Wahoo! We got one! Ladies first, Mel. Take a seat and I'll strap you in." Patrick pushed her into the chair bolted to the back of the boat as one of the crew placed a rod and reel into her hands.

She could feel the tension in the line – there was certainly something strong at the other end. The two men pulled straps across her chest and shoulders as she tried to protest.

"Don't want him pulling you overboard. There are stories of water dragons in these waters," Patrick said as he tightened the straps.

"I wouldn't blame him for not wanting to let you go. I wouldn't want to, either."

"All the water dragons in this ocean are women, Patrick. Surely you know that."

He eyed her. "How do you know that? They're pretty secretive."

Mel smiled. "Their leader is as fond of tea as I am when she's on land. A lovely lady, as long as you keep her secrets."

"So you're friends with the mermaids hereabouts, huh? We'll see by what you catch, then, I imagine." He raised his voice. "Reel him in and we'll have fresh fillets for lunch!"

Mel felt her arms tiring after ten minutes of fighting what she thought had to be a shark, it was so fierce. Patrick seemed to sense her exhaustion and he dropped to his knees behind her, his arms circling her body to help her reel in the monster fish.

"We should let him go. He fought well – for his life, Patrick. I'm tired enough to quit and admit he won. I don't need to torture this fish any more," Mel murmured.

Patrick laughed. "If we don't catch anything, there's nothing for lunch. This one will probably be all we need for the whole boat. Besides, we have to pull him up to release him from the hook. I could just cut the line, but then he'd be hurting with a barbed hook in his mouth. No, he's coming here to give you a big kiss, I'll take a picture of you and your new boyfriend, then you can decide if you want to keep him or let him go." His lips touched the base of her neck. "Have you ever had fresh wahoo, Mel?"

Mel snorted. "It sounds like something done with no clothes in the privacy of a hotel room, not on a boat full of people. I'm not answering that."

"I was going to wait until after dinner to offer my services in the privacy of your hotel room, but now works, too. Or it would if…" Two crewmen rushed forward to the port side, gaffs in hand, as Patrick slowed his reeling. "Here he comes. You caught a real monster, Mel!"

The men hauled the fish aboard and Mel let out a shocked gasp. It looked like it was longer than she was tall – and perhaps weighed more, too.

One of them knelt on the desperately fighting fish while another cut its throat. All the fight left with its spirit and tears sprang to Mel's eyes. "I take it we're not releasing him now," she said.

"No," Patrick replied. "But he'll be lunch and dinner, easy. Right – get in there with him. We need a picture of the lady who slayed the monster!" He gave her a push toward the floppy fish and pulled out his camera.

Despite her protests, the fish was lifted and arranged on the deck, so she could pull his tail up to her chest, displaying the length of him.

"Smile, Mel," Patrick coaxed and she did. The fish's spirit was in a better place now and it would be a shame to waste his sacrifice or the body he'd left behind.

"Now, the boys want photos with your monster fish, too. I think it's a record size for them and they want proof to show the other guys in the pub when they get home. Wash up and grab a drink from the cooler while I do the honours. They'll gut, fillet and cook him fresh for you – all part of the service." Patrick stared at her. "There's really nothing you can't do, is there? Charming the Indian Ocean mermaids, hooking the catch of the year, never missing a conference and…are you seriously hunting down Lucifer? He'd best watch out – he doesn't know what he's in for if you find him. Have you and Raphael…?"

Mel laughed. "Raphael and I will never fly. I think his heart's set on someone else entirely and I hope they're happy together." Patrick's face lit up and Mel impulsively kissed his cheek. "I'll go wash up," she said.

Mel used the head and started washing her hands in the tiny sink. Glancing at the even tinier mirror, she noticed a streak of blood on her shirt from the fish. She scrubbed at it but eventually gave up and returned to the deck, grateful that she'd chosen to wear her bikini under her shirt. At least the transparent cotton didn't show her underwear.

"Raphael's crazy," Patrick choked out. He couldn't seem to pull his eyes from her.

"No, Raphael's gay and in love with my brother," Mel replied gently. Her eyes searched his face. "Will you spend the evening with me? Dinner, drinks and…later, too?"

Patrick beamed. "Your wish is my command. For as long as you like."

Mel sighed inwardly even as she smiled. Patrick might have been the perfect partner if their relationship could ever be equal. As it was, though… "We have until my flight leaves tomorrow."

Twenty-nine

Mel admired the way the water cascaded over his hard body in the shower. Was it his well-muscled chest, the sculpted way the whole package was put together, or simply how well he put it to use for her pleasure? Patrick had certainly perfected both his skills and his assets over time. She could still remember the first time and how nervous he'd been…

Mel took a mouthful of water, swished it around her mouth and spat into the sink, running the tap to send the toothpaste residue down the drain.

"Say the word, Mel, and I'll transfer to Australia or wherever you're working next. All this is yours for the asking, any time you want." He gestured at his well-built body.

"You're terrified of snakes. Do you know how many reptiles we have in Australia – the really deadly kind, as well as just the cuddly ones? The closest snakeless island would be Tasmania or New Zealand. And what will happen to politics in the UK without you, Patrick? You're not just in Ireland because it's one of the few places in the world without snakes. Any time you're away, I swear violence at least doubles in the north. It seems a bit selfish to let people die just so that I can share a shower with you more than once every year or two." Mel splashed water on her face and dried it with the handtowel.

He sounded wistful. "You could move back to the UK. I'd treat you like a queen – you know that. And we'd love to have you. Politics in Europe isn't the same with this latest global financial crisis, or whatever they're calling this fit of hiccups…"

"And let Lucifer run rampant over Australia

in the meantime? I'm where I need to be, as are you. I've been working in the Indo-Pacific region for a long time now and I can't just up and leave." Mel paused to take a deep breath. She hadn't meant to sound so sharp. She exhaled, long and slow, before saying, "We have responsibilities, Patrick – and personal relationships always come second to those. We're angels – this world must come first. No matter how irresistible you are in the shower." Her cheeks heated with a faint blush that she couldn't blame on the steam in the hotel bathroom.

"I think you should come first and let the rest of the world handle itself for just a day." His grin was dirty as he rubbed soap down his thighs. He straightened and threw the bar into the dish, reaching for the shampoo instead. "I've never seen you so worried without a world war or major disaster to deal with. If you spread your spirit too thin, doing too much, you'll need to heal in Heaven until you regain your strength. Does Raphael know how stressed you are? This Lucifer thing is really getting to you, isn't it?"

Mel watched as Patrick leaned back to rinse his hair, his hips thrust forward to maintain his balance. He certainly beat any image search on her office computer and he didn't make her think of socks.

"Mel?"

She shook her head to clear it a little, wondering if it was possible for the steam to leak into her brain through her ears. Her head certainly felt misty enough. "Raphael's worried, too, and he's trying to get more angels into Western Australia, but there are so few of us there. I mean, it's so far from anywhere, which is probably why Luce chose it. That and the resources he'll control. And if it's as close to Hell as you say, that only makes the situation more serious, because he'll have as many demon reinforcements as he needs to take his corporation global. Lucifer's the key to this – I know he is – but if I tell Raphael that he'll panic and pull out. Try to pull me out. I don't know that we'll get another chance at this and it looks like it's going to have to be me." Mel looked up to meet Patrick's sympathetic eyes. "Demons. I've never dealt with demons before. I feel if I understood them, I'd have a better idea of what's going on."

"Hey, I'm not a demon expert, but if I can help…" Patrick held out his hands in an unmistakeable invitation. Mel wished she could take his offer more seriously, but his lack of clothing was decidedly distracting. "Call me – or get Raphael to call me, if you're too busy. I downloaded all yesterday's photos onto your little laptop, so you'll even have those to remind you to call me if you need me. You know I'd do anything for you."

Mel smiled and nodded. She did know – but that didn't help. "I don't want to think about Lucifer or demons again until I'm home. That'll be tonight or the early hours of tomorrow morning and plenty soon enough. Thank you for the offer and if I need you, I will call. Right now…" She sighed deeply.

Patrick's reflection winked at her in the mirror. "You know, we still have a couple of hours before I have to leave for the airport. If you want to do more than just look, there's room in this shower for two of us and there's always the bed…"

She laughed, lifting her dress over her head before dropping it on the side of the bathtub. "We shouldn't use the shower. Wouldn't want to waste all that water…"

"The water's not wasted if I'm with you," Patrick replied, pulling her into the hot water with him. "Every drop and every second is precious with you, *Mel meum*." His hands and kisses helped her forget everything but him.

"Mmm, I miss Latin. So sweet to hear it from you…" Mel closed her eyes as she let her fingers roam.

"*Quid ego faciam tibi, Mel meum?*"

(What will I do for thee, O my honey?)

Thirty

All too soon Mel found herself back at her HELL Corporation desk. Even as she returned to the task at hand, Patrick remained a warm, if receding, memory. She took one look at her long list of emails and decided to send the few pictures Patrick had taken to those she knew in the office who might care. She plugged in the memory stick with her photos and heaved a big sigh as she started on the boring backlog.

"Jez has just come through with the final pictures. Can you take a look, Mel?" Lili's voice roused Mel from trying to decipher her emails.

She wasn't the only one who'd been playing with fish and photos: someone had taken their fetish for 007 a little too far – to the point where they'd stuck a fish in a suit and called the poor thing 'James Pond'.

Lili's head popped over the partition. "Oh, good, you're already reading it. Can you print some colour copies and take it up to Luce to see what he thinks?"

Mel looked at the silly picture. "Of what?"

Lili sounded impatient. "The fish in the suit. That one!" She pointed at the screen.

Surely she couldn't be serious – it looked too silly, Mel thought, but she printed the pages anyway. She brought the papers to Lili. "You want me to take these to Luce?"

"Yes," Lili snapped. "They're the graphics for his presentation on our new Water Unit in the Environment Division. The state government wanted more money to fund the politicians' pay rise so they sold all water, fishing and boating services to us. Luce needs the pictures for our end-of-year staff talk this afternoon. Take them to him right now so we have time to get back to Jez with any changes."

Mel reminded herself for the millionth time that her job was to execute orders. "Sure," she replied, and took the photos upstairs to Luce.

Luce's personal assistant sat perkily at the desk outside his office, guarding it like a lair once again. "Can I help you?" Mephi asked sweetly.

"Hi, Lili sent me with the Water Unit pictures?" Mel let the statement become a question.

"Go on in – he's expecting you." Mephi gave Mel a professional smile before dismissing her with disinterest.

Mel stepped hesitantly into the office, glancing at the bright paintings she itched to get a closer look at.

Luce raised his eyebrows as she entered and watched her without saying a word.

Mel found his scrutiny sleazy as Hell, but she resisted the urge to pull her skirt down so that she showed as little flesh as possible. He made her feel like a million spiders were scuttling across her skin.

There had to be something about the man that was good, she told herself. The pride he took in his appearance, perhaps. His restraint in managing not to proposition her the second she walked in, despite his obvious desire to do so. The fact that he didn't smell of sulphur and brimstone. Mel took a deep breath, appreciating whatever aftershave he used to fend off the whiff of Hell.

"I brought you the pictures for your presentation," Mel began, proffering the pages. "I…hope you like them." And let me leave quickly, she added in her head.

Luce picked up the sheaf of paper and spread them across the desk. "What do you think of these?" he asked.

"I…" Mel started to say, wondering how to tell him she'd thought they were a joke without making Jez and Lili look bad.

"I think they're shit. I asked for photos that show all the good things about water that we want to preserve. Not fish in clothes pretending to be spies. Bring me something better and next time, don't waste paper. Just email them so I can post them straight into my presentation." Luce glared at her, sweeping the papers into a pile and dumping them in his bin.

Mel backed away, biting her lip hard to hide her smile. For the first time, she agreed with the demon, but she didn't dare tell him. She wondered why he employed graphic designers who couldn't follow simple instructions. Perhaps it was just Jez. Or was it a demon thing – the inability to do a job well?

She sat down heavily in her desk chair, which made her feel penitent when it squeaked in protest. She tried to distract herself by looking at her holiday photos and emailing them out before she had to tell Jez the bad news. She couldn't work out who to send them to, so she just dumped her very small contacts list in the address box and hoped she hadn't missed anyone. "A little tropical sunshine to help brighten your day," she murmured as she typed the words.

Mel hit 'send' just as the phone rang. She spent the next three hours trying to work out who was responsible for dealing with illegal dumping of dead cane toads on the front steps of some monument. She tried the Wildlife Unit, but was told that the toads were pests and they only dealt with native animals. She tried the Pest Unit, but they shooed her away like a blowfly, telling her that she could keep her dead toads or throw them in the rubbish. She went to the Lands Division, searching for someone who dealt with landfills and recycling. She was told not to waste their time. She tried to contact the building cleaner, who told her to clean up her own messes – they only cleaned the inside of the building.

In despair, she turned to Lili, who was pulling on her suit jacket. "Are you ready?" Lili asked.

Mel shook her head. "I don't know what to do."

"Come upstairs. We have the CEO's end-of-year briefing. The one with Jez's brilliant fish campaign." Lili rubbed her hands together in excitement.

Mel's heart felt like it was sliding through her ribs and out the bottom of her skirt. In all the excitement about cane toads, she'd forgotten to call Jez. "Ah, about the fish…"

Lili threaded her way through the cubicle maze to the lifts, apparently not even listening.

Mel gave up and followed her. She

wondered if she'd get to see Luce throw a tantrum this time. She resolved to sit up the back and look as small as possible. Let him take his wrath out on a demon who deserved it instead of her. Except that she felt she did deserve it this time. The cane toads had taken over…

Mel chose a seat in the highest row at the back of the seminar room, hidden behind the tallest man she could find. Lili arranged herself in the seat beside her, leaning over to speak with the tall man. He inclined his head toward Lili so Mel had a clear view of the front where Luce stood at the lectern, his presentation on the screen beside him.

He started to speak about drinking water quality and how important it was. Mel lost all interest when the first slide appeared – a picture of her drinking her third large vodka and lemonade at the hotel bar in the garden, laughing. She figured there was some water in there somewhere – perhaps in the ice.

"…stunning natural waters…."

Mel winced at the photo of her emerging from the pool. Patrick had captured the moment perfectly.

"…fun fishing opportunities…"

Mel covered her face as she saw the wahoo against her wet shirt, his tail nestled between her breasts.

"…and beautiful beaches."

At least the sunset had looked nice – it had been a wonderful walk and the weather had been warm enough to do it in just a swimsuit. Mel vowed to throw her white bikini out as soon as she got home. She hadn't realised how revealing it was until it was magnified on the presentation screen to twice life size.

"Thank you," Luce finished, as everyone clapped. He smiled straight at Mel.

She sank down in her seat. Somehow, she'd sent the CEO her holiday snaps and now everyone knew what she looked like near-naked. Heaven help her, she pleaded in her head, hoping no one heard.

Thirty-one

Mel had just started reading a new book on vampires, not her usual taste, but it was terribly compelling, so she decided to take out her phone so she could read a little more at lunch. She'd just reached the point where the vampire arrived in Hell at the call of a particularly seductive demon who seemed to be wearing nothing but a blanket…Mel was feeling unusually warm when she heard a voice.

"Mel?" Lili's head popped over the partition.

No, Callie. She wanted to know what Callie would do with…Mel tried to cool her blushing cheeks as she looked up at Lili, reluctantly putting her phone down. "Yes?"

"We've decided to move your desk. You'll be in with the rest of the team. Won't that be fun?"

She wouldn't be reading the rest of this story at work, then, Mel thought but didn't say. Callie and Lucien would have to wait until she took her train home. Unless they were going to test the bedsprings. Lucien sounded like the energetic type. Perhaps she should wait until she got home…

"Sure." Mel summoned a smile. "I'll ask the IT guys to switch my computer over, then I'll start moving my things."

Mel had to shift a surprising number of cabinets to reach the desk – they appeared to be nesting beneath and around it. After translocating the stacks of files that had migrated to the desk during its vacancy and removing the choking layer of dust, Mel looked for the computer. She saw the monitor, mouse and keyboard, but nothing else.

With a sigh, brushing the dust bunnies from her breasts, Mel trudged back to her old desk beside the fire escape. There was no response from IT. She headed across the office to the cubicles where the IT staff holed up, insulated by boxes of computer hardware beside the frozen core of the office computer servers, blinking behind the glass that made up one wall. The imps were nowhere in sight.

All the desks were empty bar one. "Yes?" the man seated at it asked. His eyes were on his screen and not on her.

"They're shifting me to the dusty desk by the big south window and I need your help setting up the computer," Mel said.

He turned slowly to face her, taking her in with an extended glance that ended in surprise when Nybbas met her eyes. "Mel!"

Mel wished she'd worn something with a longer skirt. Why did male demons always seem to stare at her legs?

"You should be fine setting it up all by yourself. I know how good you are," he said with a shy smile. "If you need a little more authority with the printers and the like, I'd be happy to help. I'll stop by and see how you're doing later on today." He gave her a pointed look and returned to his own computer in what was clearly a dismissal.

Mel sighed and returned to her computer conundrum. It had to be here somewhere…

She followed the monitor and keyboard cables to a hole in the desk surface, then tracked them to a tiny, dusty shelf in the deepest, darkest corner beneath the desk. Swearing under her breath, Mel dropped to her knees and crawled under the desk. The dust bunnies under there used growth hormones, she was certain of it.

She brushed them aside, hoping they didn't use spiders as sentries, and tried to pull the whole unit out into the light where she could see it. She was surprised to find she held a laptop on a cardboard box.

She could hear someone calling her name from behind her and she carefully backed up and out from under the desk. She was still on her hands and knees when he spoke again.

"Oh, no worries, it looks like you're doing just fine. You don't need my help." Nybbas' feet moved away from her. "Give me a shout when you want me." He walked away.

By the time Mel had managed to get to her feet, clutching the dusty laptop, she was alone. She looked down and realised that Nybbas had caught an eyeful of lace that no one should have seen. At least she'd been wearing stockings today. She smoothed her dress down over her hips and hoped he hadn't noticed.

She finished setting up the computer with the promised lack of problems, before she left for the day. As she crossed the road, she realised that the big south window was entirely transparent. The whole street and the admiring guy in the office over the road had seen a clear view of her stockings and more while she'd been under the desk.

Thirty-two

Entirely uncomfortable, with a storm brewing in her head to match the clouds above, Mel boarded a train and mentally dared anyone to even approach her with a briefcase today. No one did. When she left the train at her station, she chose to walk home instead of taking the bus. Nothing like exercise to release pent-up frustration.

She lengthened her stride as she saw the dark clouds, hoping to make it home before the rain hit. Thunder boomed above her, adding to her discomfort in the high humidity that reminded her of Singapore and Sri Lanka.

An actinic flash of lightning touched the tarmac, not fifteen metres from her. Mel looked warily at the street and the nearby trees before quickening her pace. Walking home in an electrical storm wasn't the safest thing to do.

Another flash jumped between two clouds above her head. She looked up to see the clouds actually roiling – something she didn't think real clouds did. The only time she'd ever seen clouds do that was when she'd touched Luce – the stormy shroud surrounding his soul. In fact, if she looked closely, this storm appeared to have eyes – two of them, glaring angrily down at her, just like Luce did when he wanted to blame her for something.

She shook herself. Storms only had one eye and that was calm, not angry. She must be imagining such things – two angry eyes in a storm. Preposterous!

A streak of lightning touched the road, now only ten metres from her feet. She took a deep breath, inhaling sharp ozone from the discharge. Her heels tapped frantically on the pavement as she hurried for home.

Idly, she wondered if there was a better way to relieve anger than her misguided walk. Though she wasn't the type to hurl thunderbolts at unsuspecting humans, today she felt she could do with a little target practice, especially if her target was an empty road. It might help her to release a little steam after the stressful day.

On the footpath, she bumped into a man she'd seen before, but had never come close to.

"Hello." He beamed at her.

"Hi," Mel replied, flustered. "I'm sorry…"

"Beautiful weather, don't you think?" he asked. "I'm Jimmy. What's your name?"

"Mel."

"Ah, beautiful like you, Belle," he said, holding out a full-blown, red rose, thorns and all. "For you."

She carefully took the flower from the strange man, thanking him. Both walked on in opposite directions. Mel glanced back, but he'd already disappeared. So had the angry eyes in the sky.

Perhaps hurling thunderbolts might be a better release than going for a walk, but she didn't feel the need to direct any today. Maybe another day, Mel decided.

She turned onto her street as the skies opened, showering her with warm rain. She kept walking, not caring as the precipitation pelted her, for she was already soaked in sweat from the sweltering heat of the day. Any other wetness was an improvement.

She stepped inside, dripping across the carpet, heading for the kitchen to take care of the rose. Mature and red, both the lovely fragrance and defensive spikes marked it as a rose from a garden and not a florist. What was it supposed to mean? Was there some strange symbolism she was supposed to see? Or was it simply a lovely gift to remind her that there was more to life than HELL?

She placed the rose in a pint glass of water. Maybe she could look into learning to throw lightning from on high next week. She was sure some new situation at work would inspire her.

Thirty-three

Mel checked the weather forecast before she hopped into the shower. It said cool with the chance of a shower and lengthy fine periods, but outside it looked like a perfect day that was heating up the way it always did in summer. She put out pants and a skirt and resolved to check the sky once more before she dressed. She didn't want a repeat of yesterday's drenching on her way to work today.

The fine sky and dark forecast hadn't changed. She tried to decide between the slim-fitted pants and the light skirt that flared nicely as she moved. In the end, Mel gave in and chose both. The pants first, the skirt over the top. If it was still hot when she got to work, she'd stick with the long skirt, but if it had cooled a bit, she'd take the skirt off and show off her new pants. She vowed not to give the people on the plaza another view they wouldn't forget.

She set off for the train station, the skirt swirling a little in the light north-westerly. The clouds for the promised shower had appeared on the horizon behind her, but she had an umbrella, so she ignored them and kept going.

She was perhaps five minutes from the train station when the skies opened in a brief downpour. She unfolded her umbrella and kept walking, knowing it would end soon, as it always did.

The umbrella kept her hair dry, but the light breeze had grown and the water came at her sideways. The umbrella was no use and the lovely skirt caught the wind and rain with equal greed. By the time Mel reached the train station, her skirt was soaked through and clinging to her legs. Her pants were drinking the water in her skirt like a man determined to find a cure for his hangover.

Bedraggled, Mel thought about heading home for a change of clothes, but that would make her late, so she made her way to the platform and caught the next train into the city. The other passengers avoided her as she fanned her dripping skirt out, trying to dry it.

By the time the train arrived, she was no longer dripping, but Mel was still very soggy. Her shoes squelched with each step from the station to HELL.

On the plaza and the street in front of the office, Mel found hundreds of construction workers in fluorescent shirts, protesting about the lack of local labour employed on a particular mining construction project. She squeezed her way through the angry men, wishing her pale pastels didn't stand out so much in a sea of fluorescent yellow and orange.

Once in the office, she breathed a sigh of relief as she sank into her desk chair, switching on her computer. It was a few seconds before she realised the water in her skirt and pants was quickly wicking into her underwear. She stood and headed for the toilets to do something about it.

Gerry saw her hurry past and commented, "You look wet. Did you get caught in the rain?"

Mel stopped and nodded. "Soaked through."

"Didn't you bring an umbrella or a change of clothes?" he asked sympathetically.

Mel blushed. "I had an umbrella, but it didn't do much, and I didn't plan on needing a change of clothes…"

Lili's head popped up above her partition. "Oh, I keep a spare pair of pants for after-work parties, in case I…" She trailed off and flashed a suggestive smile. "You can borrow them if you like."

Mel smiled at Lili. "Thank you, but I'll be all right."

Inwardly, she shuddered at the thought of wearing Lili's pants without her underwear. That would be terribly awkward, she felt. Not to mention the rumour that Lili was Lucifer's mistress – given Luce evidently slept around a bit, or attempted to, he'd probably been in those pants on numerous occasions.

Gerry looked worried. "Now, you know you'll feel better if you take all that wet gear off." He smiled kindly. "You really should take it all off and take up Lili's offer."

Lili nodded vigorously. "You really should."

Mel managed a sickly smile in response as she shook her head. "Thank you, but…"

Gerry grinned. "I'll just keep telling you to take your skirt off 'til you do."

A shriek split the air. Mephi stood with both hands to her mouth, staring from Gerry to Mel. "That's sexual harassment. Don't you give in to him and take your skirt off, dear. I'll report him directly!" Mephi hurried off into the ladies' loo. Gerry followed her, protesting his innocence.

Mel turned and walked as quickly as she could back to her office, shutting the door behind her. She shared it with three other people, but they weren't in yet. Resigned, she knew the ladies' loo was out, so she was glad she had the office to herself.

With her eyes fixed on the door to make

sure no one came in, she shimmied out of her wet pants and underwear, leaving just a skirt clinging damply to her skin. She fanned it out, trying to dry it as much as possible.

A loud cheer floated up from the protesters outside and she turned around to see what had happened. They all looked like they were staring at her building. Maybe someone had unrolled a banner down the side, in support of their cause. She shrugged and spread her skirt out to its fullest as she sat down, turning her computer on and staring at the screen.

Down below, the protesters made unhappy sounds and started to move away from the plaza. She watched them go, for once pleased by the good view offered by her window. When the men had marched out of sight up the Terrace, she looked down at her skirt to see if it had dried at all. Silhouetted between the office lights and the window, she realised the lavender skirt was transparent.

"Oh Hell," said Mel. She really wished she'd worn stockings today.

Thirty-four

"…meeting at seven," Lili's voice said.

Mel struggled to remember why she was dreaming about Lili, as she was certain she was at home in bed. It was definitely dark. "Mmmph?"

A sigh of exasperation. "There's been an incident and Luce has called an emergency meeting. You've been tapped to take the meeting minutes, so you'll need to be in at work before the meeting at seven. I had to call your agency to put me through to you, because they wouldn't give me your direct number, so

I've wasted enough time already. Get in here."

"Yeah, okay," Mel mumbled. The phone beeped in her ear as Lili hung up. That was enough to wake Mel properly.

Half an hour later, showered, styled and squeezed into a suit, Mel trudged to the train station. She could see the sun just rising behind the building, like the sky was on fire. Pretty, she thought muzzily, stumbling down the stairs to the train at the platform.

Despite the early hour, the train was fairly full, but Mel managed to find one of the last free seats. She sank down onto her seat and pulled out her smartphone. She'd found a romance story set in the aftermath of the American Civil War that looked interesting and indeed it was. She was soon engrossed.

The train pulled up at the next station and another herd of commuters boarded, squeezing in like sardines. The doors closed and the train started to move. One woman, looking as sleepy as Mel felt, didn't hold on to anything and lost her balance. She stumbled into Mel as she tried to regain her footing, but the train lurched and tipped her again. This time she fell face-first into Mel's lap.

Mel opened her mouth to ask if the poor woman was okay, but she was silenced by the sound of Nybbas' voice as he caught sight of her. "Ooh, hello!" he boomed, his eyes widening as he took in the sight of Mel with another woman draped across her lap.

Laughter erupted among the commuters and Mel felt her face redden, as did the other woman, who quickly picked herself up and squeezed between people to put as much distance between herself and Mel as she could.

She and Nybbas detrained at the same station. He walked beside her all the way to the office.

Nyybas had a broad smile on his face, looking far too alert for Mel's foggy mind. "I didn't know you liked eating out for breakfast."

Mel thought about the raspberry yoghurt she hadn't had time for that morning. "This morning's special," she replied, inhaling the waft of bacon perfume emanating from a plaza café.

"I'd love to have breakfast with you one day then," Nybbas returned.

Mel smiled. "How about after this morning's meeting? I have a craving for bacon."

Nybbas seemed stunned by her invitation. "S-s-sure," he stammered.

Thirty-five

"Right, take your coffee. Time to start this meeting," Luce said, waving his hand at the tray of steaming cups that Mephi held. Mel concentrated on powering up her laptop, knowing Mephi would never make a coffee for her.

"Mel," she heard Luce say. She glanced up to see him jerk his head at the remaining cup on the tray. It was hers – no one else here owned a white and gold mug, and the white-hearted macchiato it contained was unmistakeable. Luce must have made Mephi do it – unless he'd made the coffee himself. She smiled her thanks as she took the mug. So sweet of him to remember.

Mel sipped her fresh-brewed coffee between typing, savouring the flavour.

"When was it found?"

"On the twentieth of October."

"Why haven't we acted on it before now? That was over a month ago!"

"She contacted us to tell us about it, but gave us the wrong phone number and never told us any more. We didn't know how to get in contact with her."

"Why did you bring it up now?"

"She sent us photos and it looks suspicious."

"Where is it? What happened to it?"

"She stored it in the freezer."

Alien invasion commenced on 20/10, Mel typed. **Member of the public found body, reported find but couldn't be contacted. Alien body photographed and stored in freezer for further investigation.**

"Why don't we have the body?"

"We've sent one of our staff to retrieve it.

He was due there at seven, when the meeting started, so he'll contact us once he's identified and secured the specimen."

The phone rang. Luce hit the speakerphone button.

"Hello? Report."

"Luce, this is Jez from PR. We have enquiries from all the main media channels, requesting a press conference with you regarding the alien invasion."

"Ah."

"The online news sites are already running a story about the invasion. We need to comment as soon as possible."

CEO to give immediate press conference to prevent panic, Mel typed.

"Set it up for half an hour? I need to go find a tie." Luce left.

About five minutes after his departure, the phone rang again. Lili hit the speakerphone button, trying to sound as authoritative as Luce. "Hello? Report."

"Hi, it's Phil. We have one specimen, but the other one is gone."

"You've lost an alien?"

"No, not entirely. We know where it is. The alien was mistaken for seafood at a barbeque and met with an unfortunate accident."

Mel's fingers skittered across the keys. **Alien corpse bbqed and served at a party.**

"What happened?"

"Ah, the lady who found it says that it was quite delicious. She gave us the remains of the carcass."

"Can you identify it?"

"It appears to bear some similarity to a local tropical rock lobster species…"

Tropical rock lobster mistaken for alien – report is a false alarm, Mel typed as fast as she could.

"What about the remaining specimen?"

"Definitely a very large tropical rock lobster. We've commandeered the specimen for testing…one of our researchers would like to see what it tastes like with butter."

"Ah, okay. Thanks, Phil."

"Sure, bye."

Relieved murmurs flowed around the table. Everyone else started discussing where they intended to go for breakfast following the meeting.

"Um, Lili?" Mel ventured. "What are we going to tell the press conference?"

Lili smiled, her handbag already on her shoulder as she straightened her shirt in preparation for going out. "It's not the end of the world. Just step upstairs and tell Luce it was a false alarm. He can tell the media that we've averted disaster." She followed the team out toward the lift.

Mel broke into a run up the stairs to the seminar room, where Luce had held the briefing on her in her bikinis. She could hear the sound of voices behind the door, so she silently turned the handle and slipped inside.

At the front, his gaze sweeping a dozen cameras as he spoke into a myriad of microphones, Luce smiled. "The important thing to remember is that, even if aliens are invading and the apocalypse is nigh, this is not the end of the world. We have specialist staff ready to respond to any and all invasion forces…" He caught sight of her. "Yes?"

All eyes and lenses turned to Mel and her insides froze with fear, as they always did when she had to speak in public.

Mel dropped to her knees. It might not be an alien invasion, but it was the end of the world. Her boss had just predicted doomsday from an invasion of lobsters. She didn't dare say that the specialist staff were responding with butter. She couldn't say a word. Oh Hell.

The crowd seemed to surge closer to her with a concerned cacophony of sound, but Luce held up his hands for silence and space as he strode closer. "Are you here to report that the situation has been contained?" Luce asked tersely.

Mutely, Mel nodded. Contained in a steamer, she couldn't seem to say. Tears sprang to her eyes and trickled down her cheeks.

"One of our dedicated staff, ladies and gentlemen, who played a key role in averting disaster." Luce leaped lightly up the steps and held out a hand to Mel. She grasped his arm as she rose, holding on to him for support. All she could feel emanating from him was sympathy – a strange sensation for a demon, she thought, as she permitted him to lead her forward to the lectern. "May I present the heroine who's saved the day, Miss Melody Angel!" he boomed, a supportive arm sliding around her waist when it felt like she'd fall to her knees again. Flashes blinded her, shimmering through her tears.

"No further questions," Luce said, waving them away with his free hand. He stood at Mel's side until the last journalist had left, shutting the door behind him. The unusually solicitous demon helped her sit in one of the front-row chairs.

Mel stared at Luce, trying to work out what motivated this sudden change. First the coffee, now this…what did he want?

He handed her a black cotton handkerchief. "That's the second time this week you've saved me from embarrassment in this room. Thank you, angel."

Mel cleared her throat. "Mel. My name is Mel."

"I know your name. Now, so do all of the media."

Mel smiled wanly, passing his damp handkerchief back. "Great. Please forgive me if I don't thank you for that."

Luce frowned. "But the situation is contained, isn't it? And you are the one who was sent with the good news?"

Mel nodded. "Yes, but…"

"That makes you the heroine who single-handedly saved us all from an alien invasion, as well as me from some hard-to-answer questions. It seems I'm in your debt, Mel. All of us are." He met her eyes. "I hope you intend to stay with the corporation for a while. We could use more staff like you."

"I did nothing but take the minutes in the meeting, and it turned out that the emergency was a false alarm," Mel said steadily. "Anyone could have done what I did."

Luce shrugged. It looked like he was trying to hide a smile. "So what would you have done if I'd given you a choice? Announced that I was an idiot, or agreed to be the heroine of the HELL Corporation? You had the chance to tell them yourself."

Tell all those reporters, with their cameras, that Luce was an idiot? Mel felt her will drain from her at even the thought of the audience. No, she couldn't have said it – even if it had been true, which it wasn't. And now Luce knew her weakness – her fear of public speaking. She bet he found it funny as Hell.

"Are you feeling okay?" He looked uncertain. "Do you need a hand getting up, or…"

Mel waved him away and rose. "I'll be fine." She trudged up the steps, putting as much distance as she could between herself and the strange demon.

"Remember, I owe you!" he called after her.

And one day, she'd collect, she resolved, but not today.

Thirty-Six

Mel sipped her morning macchiato as she checked her emails, wishing she was reading that book she'd found over breakfast, the one about reincarnation. The veiled woman on the cover had looked so mysterious…

"Mel, we're getting lots of calls at Reception on the new legislation. We need you to help field enquiries," Lili said without warning.

Mel looked up, stunned. "What about the alien invasion? Aren't I supposed to stay away from the public after I cried in the press conference?"

Lili shrugged. "Luce took care of that. He put out a media release that the invasion had been contained and we'd remain vigilant. No mention of what species they were. He just called you a 'dedicated member of staff' who had 'worked tirelessly to manage the incursion.' He thinks the photos of you in the paper in tears were brilliant. He specifically requested you to help with enquiries."

Mel sighed. At least on Reception she could take her phone with her and read that story between calls. She slipped the smartphone into her pocket, gulped down the last of her coffee and straightened her shirt. "Sure. What questions will I have to answer?"

Lili handed over a booklet. "The new legislation that came into effect on the first. People have lots of questions and they're all answered in this."

Mel took the booklet and smiled as she headed out to Reception, feeling the heavy bump of the phone in her pants pocket with each step.

She sat next to another girl, who was dressed in a fresh white shirt instead of the

HELL Corporation uniform. The girl clunked her phone down before burying her face in her hands.

Mel introduced herself. "Here to help," she added.

"No, I'm here to help," the girl said, a slightly hysterical edge to her voice. "I'm Gabrielle, from Helpful Angels, temporarily here to take phone enquiries. What have I been volunteered for? This is really hard." She turned to face Mel and her eyes widened with recognition. "What are you doing here? Raphael said you were in India or something…"

Mel smiled. "Nope, I'm back and it looks like they've given us the worst job they can think of – ah, it'll be easy for a couple of angels, you'll see. Welcome to HELL. It's not too bad, once you get used to it."

Gabi shrugged. "I probably won't be here that long."

The phone rang and Gabi answered it, turning away. She looked pained.

Mel's phone rang, too, so she took a deep breath and answered it. "Good morning,

HELL Corporation. How may I help?"

"This is shit."

Mel fought not to laugh. "What is, sir?"

"The new changes to the laws. We're the Cane Toad Action Group and according to the new animal welfare laws, we can't kill any animal in the State without it being done by an authorised veterinarian. It's BULLSHIT."

Mel agreed with him so she tried to be soothing. "Surely that can't be right. I'm sure the new animal welfare laws were only changed to… 'better protect native species, pets and stock.'" She read the list quickly off the front of the brochure, hoping he wouldn't notice her hesitation.

"Well someone better fix this then, because I'm not going to get a vet to personally kill a thousand cane toads. First, I'm going to ring my mate, who's a reporter with Channel Six. Then, I'm going to put the buggers in a bag and gas them the same as we always do…and you can tell your fucking policy people they're stupid!" The irate man hung up.

Mel made a note of the man's point and picked up the brochure with a sigh. Surely no one could write legislation that protected cane toads from being killed. They were a noxious pest that had to be neutralised on sight…

The phone rang again. This time the enquirer was female. "I have a question about the new laws."

Please don't let it be about cane toads, Mel prayed.

The woman's voice shook. "I have a redback spider in my house and I'm terrified it will bite my dog or me, but my neighbour told me that the new laws mean I can't kill it. I can't afford to get a vet out here to do it. What do I do? I don't want it to kill me…"

Mel privately thought she would have preferred cane toads. "I'm sure the laws don't cover redback spiders. You just spray it, squish it or shift it outside, like you would normally."

The woman sniffled as she agreed to do what Mel said, before ending the call.

Gabi was looking at Mel as she hung up. "So, what's the deal with this legislation?" Mel asked, feeling that she'd been dropped into something she hadn't agreed to.

Gabi's expression darkened. She reached for

Mel's brochure, flipping quickly through the pages. "The animal rights activists managed to push through this new legislation, which apparently applies to 'all non-human animals in the state' where they must die a humane death, as administered by an authorised vet. The first query I got was about rats, the next was about fishing…and the list just grows. Apparently you can't kill the fish you've caught without a vet, you can't poison rats, can't spray flies and your pet fish can't die of natural causes…and whoever wrote this isn't living in the real world."

Mel started to laugh. "Well, they'll just have to change it to say some animals are exempt from the law, right?"

Gabi shook her head. "They probably will, but it won't be today. Until they do, we'll be dealing with all the questions."

"Excuse me, ladies," a sleazy voice said.

Don't let it be Luce, Mel prayed. The last thing she needed was for Gabi to positively identify him as Lucifer and throw the office into chaos.

Both Gabi and Mel looked up, eyebrows

raised.

"I couldn't help but overhear," the stranger said smoothly, "but is it true that the new legislation is a little, ah, problematic and short-sighted?"

Mel found this smarmy stranger familiar. "Legislation is law. What else it is I'd say is up to the policy makers who have to deal with it." She looked hard at him. "Can I help you?"

"I'm from Channel Six news and I've come to interview your CEO about the new legislation. He's expecting me." He grinned greasily at Mel.

She suppressed a shudder, changing her mind and wishing the man had been Luce instead. This must have been one of the reporters at the press conference where she'd cried. Gabi was already on the phone, nodding as she spoke to Mephi. "You can go on in."

Mel jumped to her feet, hoping to keep Gabi away from Luce for a little longer. "I'll take you up to his office." She led the way to the stairs.

Luce smiled at the sight of her and happily greeted the reporter. The two men shook hands and exchanged greetings as Mel stood in the doorway, wondering what to do next.

"We'll be fine, thank you, Mel. Can you send Mephi in to arrange coffee?" Luce asked. Both his and the reporter's eyes followed Mel as she walked out of the office. She tried to ignore their scrutiny.

Mephi huffed as she stood, having already heard Luce's words, and minced into the meeting to arrange refreshments.

As Mel headed away from the office, she heard the reporter's first question. "So, Mr Iblis, as CEO of HELL Corporation, can you tell us how this new legislation will affect containment of the alien invasion? Are we drafting an army of veterinarians to kill the alien menace?"

Mel almost choked as she headed toward the stairs, hoping to put as much distance between herself and the reporter as possible before she lost it laughing. Sometimes, working for this corporation was funny as Hell.

Thirty-Seven

"This is getting so dull, I think I need a coffee to keep me awake," Gabi muttered. "Cover for me for fifteen minutes while I go get one?"

Mel nodded as she listened to the very long story some woman seemed compelled to tell her – something about a fish in a shop's aquarium that gave her nightmares. Mel still wasn't entirely sure what the caller expected her to do about it. She evidently needed some form of counselling.

Twenty minutes later, she'd managed to end the call, hand over six visitor badges to humans who had meetings with HELL Corporation personnel, and handle two over-the-counter enquiries about payments for various licences that they had the authority to issue. She'd smiled politely three times when people recognised and congratulated her for saving them from aliens.

Longing for a coffee herself and a trip to the toilet, she waited patiently for Gabi to return. Her coffee run sure was taking a long time. Mel hoped Gabi hadn't run into Luce in the lunchroom.

She took a telephone enquiry about rain water tanks and transferred it to the demon who dealt with such things.

Luce appeared with the reporter, who winked at Mel as he handed back his visitor badge. She managed to send him on his way without her home telephone number, despite his insistence that she give it to him. She sighed and closed her eyes.

If only Luce hadn't made her out to be some sort of heroine to the press and then allowed this poorly thought-out legislation to pass, her job would be so much easier.

"Would you give me your phone number, if I asked?"

Mel opened her eyes. Luce hadn't left – he leaned against the door to the rest of the office, grinning at her.

"Sure," she replied. "As long as I'm working here in HELL..." She gave him the switchboard number for Reception – the number it seemed like every crazy human in this city had felt the need to call today.

Luce laughed. "And your personal number? The one for the mobile phone I see you reading so avidly on during your breaks, or the number for the house you take sanctuary in when your work day is done?"

"No," she replied honestly. "I don't want to be worried about work when I'm not here. Especially with this misguided new legislation. It seems everyone has a different question that wasn't considered when whichever cloistered individual wrote it. Was there no public consultation at all?"

Luce shook his head. "Nope. And cloistered individuals sound about right – the pair of angels we got from the agency before you arrived were the ones who wrote it. I don't think those two knew much about humans at all — spent too much time in Heaven, contemplating their own divinity. Holy legislation is what they've given me — in that it's full of holes."

"Angels? You mean Camael and Samael? The ones you poached from the agency? Figures. They're fine debating complicated legal points, but writing the laws in the first place? They're neither experienced nor qualified. I would have thought that your people were better at putting together legally binding agreements. Legislation shouldn't be such a big step; surely you have damned lawyers at your disposal…" Mel paused as she realised Luce was silent. "I'm sorry. It's your corporation. I'm sure you can assign whatever poorly qualified personnel you see fit to the task."

Luce laughed. "I've said it before and I'll say it again. You're not like any other angel I've ever met. Yet I'm incredibly happy we have an angel like you handling all the public enquiries on this mess. No one else could do it.

Speaking of which…isn't there meant to be another angel on Reception with you?"

"Yes." Mel sighed. "She said she was getting coffee, but it's been half an hour and she's still not back."

"I'll get you one. The least I can do in exchange for you handling this so well. I know what you like." Luce winked.

Mel couldn't help but laugh. "That would be wonderful."

She waited for one of them to return, hoping it would be soon and not at the same time. If Gabi encountered Luce over the coffee machine, she could do some serious damage with hot water and steamed milk.

Luce was back first, carrying her mug of macchiato alongside his own steaming cup. "Thank you," she said with a smile, raising her cup in salute. "Did you see Gabi in there?"

He cheerfully shook his head. "I should get back to work. I can't be making coffee all day. I have a stack of poorly punctuated reports on my desk to approve." With another wink, he disappeared through the office door.

Mel sighed, sipping her perfect coffee, as

she worried about what had happened to Gabi.

The girl herself breezed through the doors. "What kind of city doesn't have a Starbucks?" she demanded. "No one could tell me where I could get a Frappuccino…so I eventually found a place that did flavoured ice coffees with an espresso base. Look, I got a white chocolate and a French vanilla iced latte. Which one do you want?"

They both looked identical to Mel – creamy-coloured milkshakes. She still had a little of her coffee left, but she didn't want to offend Gabi, so she took the one closer to her and offered her thanks for the confection.

Mel tipped the last of her coffee into her mouth and almost choked when Gabi squealed, "How can you drink that? Is that from the demons' coffee machine? You don't know what they put in there! It could be anything…don't drink it, Mel!" She ripped the mug out of Mel's fingers. Too late – it was empty.

"They put coffee beans and milk in it," Mel protested. "Same as anyone else. It's safe, Gabi, honestly."

"But demons use it. How often would they clean a coffee maker? I'd want to disinfect the whole thing, then wash it again to get rid of the stink of corruption. They're demons – there's nothing good about them and everything they touch is tainted by the contact." She looked grim. "I don't know how you've managed to share the office with them for so long. I can barely put up with the proximity, sitting out here apart from them."

Mel's heart ached for the demons Gabi had denigrated. She knew the coffee machine was impeccably maintained – her colleagues appreciated a quality coffee more than she did. There was nothing tainted or corrupted about her coffee – Luce had made it exactly the way she liked it, as promised. She wondered what Gabi would say if she knew a demon had made the contents of her cup.

"Gabi, they're not that bad. I've met worse humans than some of the demons in this office. They were angels once, too, you know…"

Gabi snorted. "They're demons and everything about them is bad. They can't do anything good. The humans worse than them are destined to be either damned or demons themselves when they die. And they might have been angels once, but they fell for a reason. Don't let them drag you down with them. They'll do it out of sheer mischief – their desire to corrupt anything good. Just focus on what we're here for. We have to find Lucifer, find out what he's up to, and stop him. Then we can get the Hell out of here as fast as possible."

Mel sighed. She knew where he was and what he was doing, but she was happy to let Luce drink his coffee and check reports at his desk. Gabi would surely encounter him in the office soon enough. She was surprised the archangel hadn't met him already. Mel wondered if she'd be as eager to leave as Gabi.

The phone trilled and Mel picked up the receiver. "Hello, HELL Corporation. How may I…"

"They've done it again! There's a pile of dead cane toads at the bottom of the War Memorial this time! I want something done about it! Desecrating our fallen heroes' memories…"

Mel sighed. Maybe there were some things she wouldn't miss.

Thirty-eight

"Prostitutes have more jargon than I'd realised…do you know what a body slide is? Or how much they charge for one?"

Lili had to repeat her question before Mel realised she was the one being addressed.

"A…a body slide?" Mel swallowed, trying not to imagine it. "Should I know?"

Lili shrugged. "Probably not. You'd go and work in their industry instead, if you knew how much they charged."

Mel found that hard to believe. "Oh, I doubt it. I like it here," she managed to say.

Lili considered this. "Well, I guess you could be a phone sex worker. You have the voice for it. One of my friends did that for a while. She had the funniest stories…"

Mel almost choked, but recovered before Lili noticed. "No, thank you. I'm sure it doesn't pay well, and imagine what they might say!"

"You'd have a script of what to say. I'm sure it would mostly be a matter of what colour underwear to tell them you're wearing today…"

Mel spluttered into silence.

"Anyway, they don't pay us enough here," Lili concluded, to Mel's relief. "I wish some billionaire would marry me and then I wouldn't have to work any more."

Gerry's head popped up from behind a partition. "I think Ginger Rhinestone's available!" He wore a big grin.

"Is she?" Lili asked. "Hmm, I wonder…"

Mel tried to keep her breakfast down. She didn't think that Ginger Rhinestone, a particularly plump, female mining magnate, could ever have enough money to attract her. She found herself wondering how Lili could…she shook herself and hoped she'd dislodged the disturbing image, too.

"Right, they don't pay me enough to keep doing this. Come on, it's time for the Christmas party!" Lili beckoned to Mel, who followed her cautiously to the fancy hotel over the road.

They both accepted glasses of wine from the waiter at the entrance, Mel sipped slowly while Lili knocked hers back quickly so she could seize another.

Lili caught sight of a colleague she wanted to talk to and left Mel standing by the waiter. Mel breathed a sigh of relief and pulled out her phone, thinking about catching up on the story she'd been reading on the train that morning. The girl called Nona sounded nice.

…he knocked her out with what? Mel thought, feeling her face grow red.

"Mel!" Luce's smile looked happy. "Welcome to the HELL Corporation Christmas party! Now, you're not at work, so put your phone away — no working!" He reached for her phone to turn it off.

Mel swiped frantically at the screen, hoping

to wipe it of words before Luce saw what had made her blush.

She needn't have worried. He didn't even glance at it.

"I've been meaning to thank you for all your hard work and help – even letting me use your photos for my presentation. They were exactly what I needed!" He beamed at her.

"Ah, no worries," Mel replied uneasily. She slipped her phone back into her pocket.

"Have you checked where you're sitting yet?" he asked, nodding at the noticeboard.

Mel shook her head and leaned closer to look for her name.

"There you are – on my table!" Luce looked pleased, pointing, as Mel's heart sank. She wouldn't be reading anything else about Nona today.

Mel followed him into the hotel function room to their table. Christmas-coloured balloons rose from a weighted, wrapped gift in the centre. Luce insisted that she sit beside him, next to the dance floor, and she reluctantly complied. Lili slid in on her other side, followed by the other executives.

Mel grew steadily paler. She swore not to drink any more wine, lest she make a mistake. She sipped slowly from her glass and set it down.

Looking around at the room, she wondered who most of them were. Gerry and Merih joined a table which was mostly occupied by men. Other staff wandered in, chatting happily as they sat down. With a sinking heart, Mel realised that she was the only angel present.

The food was served quickly and Mel reached for her wine. Inexplicably, the glass had refilled. Another sip and she returned to her steak, careful to carve it into small pieces so she wouldn't make a fool of herself.

Dessert was a slice made of layers of raspberry and dark chocolate mousse that looked obscenely pink, even in the dim light of the function room.

"Oh, this is amazing," Lili moaned, her spoon in her mouth.

Mel looked at her in alarm, but Lili took her spoon to the mousse again with a rapt expression, in no apparent danger.

Luce's voice sounded throaty. "You have to

try this."

Moans rose from Merih and Gerry's table.

It sounded like the demons around her were all experiencing the same mass orgasm. Mel didn't know where to look, so she touched the pinkness with her fingertip and thrust it into her mouth. She closed her eyes, the better to focus on the taste without the distraction of the others around her. This pleasure was private and Mel decided she wanted more, opening her eyes and her mouth eagerly. A glance told her Luce had seen her sucking on her finger and found it funny as Hell, so she capitulated and picked up a spoon for the next taste.

She finished her dessert with reluctance, wishing there was more to prolong the pleasure. Mel reached for her wine.

It had refilled itself again, though she was sure it'd been almost empty. She shrugged and drank.

The jukebox by the dance floor increased its volume. The medley from *Grease* kicked off this party as it had every other one she'd attended since the movie had been released.

Mel waited for the next traditional song – where a man declared he'd walk five hundred miles – and was rewarded by the next track. The dance floor started to fill with her more eager colleagues, but Mel remained firmly in her seat.

A dance track began, the Korean lyrics surprising her. Something about a warm girl who liked coffee. The dance floor cleared quickly, leaving only eight women, who began to dance with a synchronicity that spoke of practice.

Mel felt her jaw drop. She was sure she'd never seen a version of *Gangnam Style* where the girls rode on female horses who evidently enjoyed the experience. It looked like they were all equipped with items she'd seen in that adult shop up the road, too…

"Aren't they brilliant?" Luce shouted in her ear, over the music. He refilled her glass as he spoke.

"I…" Mel swallowed. "Isn't this one of those things that the company calls inappropriate behaviour? I could lose my job if someone from the Human Resources

Department finds out I've been looking at this!"

Luce laughed. "I keep forgetting you're not one of my staff and you still work for the agency – if you'd ever had to put in a leave form or ask about a payslip, you'd know that they are the HR Department – the manager is riding the rather well-endowed horse in the middle. I think she'd prefer you just sit down and watch the show, and applaud loudly afterwards."

Mel regarded the dancing demons. It looked like the horses wore some sort of saddle with odd protuberances strapped on to them. She wondered how anyone was supposed to comfortably ride…

Mel groped blindly for her wine glass with her eyes squeezed tightly shut. Perhaps if she drank enough, she'd manage to forget what she'd just seen her colleagues do.

Thirty-nine

"Time for the Christmas party!" Lili sang out. "Computers off – you won't be coming back today!"

Mel stared. "I thought we already had the office Christmas party. The one at the hotel, with the dancers and..."

Please, don't make me sit through another dance interpretation of *Gangnam Style*, she prayed silently. She still wished she didn't know what a double delight strap-on was for.

"Of course we did. That was the whole office. This is just our unit – we're going down to Matilda Bay with the swans for a barbeque."

"We're eating swan?" Mel asked, horrified. After the exotic dancers from HR, nothing would surprise her about office Christmas parties in HELL.

Lili laughed. "No, but they might try and eat us. Gerry got us some steaks and sausages, Ana and Merih have some salads, Gabi is bringing the rolls and I took care of the drinks. Time to make merry, Mel!"

Mel conceded the point and proceeded to shut down her computer. Sausages, swans and steak. It wasn't that heavenly mousse, but it was still a celebration and she wouldn't miss it. Demons celebrating Christmas – who'd have thought? "How are we getting there?" she asked.

"A few of us are driving over to the foreshore. I can give you a lift, if you like. I have one seat spare in my car."

Mel accepted gracefully and followed Lili to the underground car park, inexplicably burdened with more wine than she could drink. She wondered why a lot of it was bubbly and pink – it didn't seem like normal demonic fare, but who was she to judge? Her shoulders were too heavily burdened to shrug, so she kept her thoughts to herself.

Lili took the bags of bottles from her, loading them into the boot of her tiny two-seater convertible. The shiny red paintwork seemed to glow even in the dimly lit basement. Mel's fingers itched to drive Lili's car herself – it certainly looked like fun. Fleetingly, she wondered why no one else would want the passenger seat in Lili's lovely car.

"C'mon, Mel, hurry up or they'll start without us!" Lili insisted. She'd slid behind the steering wheel while Mel had mused.

Mel yanked open the door and buckled her seatbelt. She'd barely slammed the door behind her before Lili revved the engine and reversed.

Mel's question was answered quickly. Lili drove like…well, a demon, she decided. A demon with a death wish. Clinging to her seat, both feet firmly braced in the footwell as if she was braking with all her weight, she couldn't take her horrified eyes off the traffic whizzing past their erratically guided missile of a Mazda. The third time the seatbelt strained against her chest at Lili's sudden stop, Mel tried to shut the whole experience out, praying it would be over soon.

"Oh good! Merih and Gerry have already claimed us some tables!" Lili said, cracking open her door.

Mel opened her eyes and unclenched her hands from the bottom of her seat, hoping she hadn't clawed any of the upholstery off in her panic. There didn't appear to be anything unusual under her nails so she escaped from the car.

She tried to settle her shaky legs as she stepped across the grass to the table where the food was laid out. Both Merih and Gerry stood at the barbeque, each holding a beer in one hand and tongs in the other. "Is there anything I can do?" she asked.

"Nope!" Gerry grinned. "You just sit and guard the table from the hellspawn swans. Grab a drink, Mel!"

Hellspawn swans? They looked like normal black swans, Mel thought, examining the large birds by the water's edge. Surely a demon wouldn't blink at hellspawn, no matter what shape it took…

Lili pushed a plastic goblet of pink bubbly into her hand. Mel thanked her and approached the table. One swan unfolded its legs and stretched its neck in her direction, but didn't move closer.

Mel tucked her skirt beneath her and perched on the picnic bench, glancing at the food spread across the table's surface. Plenty of salad, alcohol, plates, cutlery…and some of the expensive bakery rolls she couldn't usually afford. Her stomach made its presence known as her eyes focussed on the heavily seeded rolls that were her favourite. One wouldn't hurt, she decided, slipping her fingers into the bakery bag. The top of the roll was hard to the touch, yet it yielded beneath her fingers, telling her it hadn't been sitting in the humid office all day or in a freezer for longer – this was baked fresh today and bought not long before.

"Go on," Gabi said softly, seating herself beside Mel. "I made sure to get the ones you like – and a few extra, just in case. They won't miss a couple of rolls."

Both angels looked over to the barbeque,

where it appeared Merih had poured a beer over the hotplate, sending up a mushroom cloud of steam. The loud hissing didn't drown out their raucous laughter.

Mel agreed and the paper bag crackled as she extracted her prize.

Merry Christmas to me, she thought as she bit into the crusty roll, crunching through the seeds in bliss.

A high-pitched honk, like the squeak of a clarinet, drove her eyes open. The swan's red and white beak was level with her knees as he cocked his head so his red-ringed eye could make contact with hers.

"You want some of this roll, too? I don't blame you," Mel told him, breaking off a bite-sized piece and holding it before his beak. The swan took the morsel without touching her fingers. As Mel took another large bite, she almost choked with laughter as the swan lifted his head to look for more. Swallowing, she broke off another bit for the bird.

Together, they finished the roll and the swan seemed as eager as Mel for another. Without taking her eyes off the bird, Mel asked, "Gabi, is there any chance I could have another one?"

Paper crackled and something hard, rough and seedy touched her elbow. Mel reached over to take it and her fingers grazed those wrapped around the roll.

Dark clouds roiled, the sort only seen in a seriously strong storm – or surrounding a severely troubled soul. Yet this storm had an eye, a break through which she could see…

"You're not Gabrielle," Mel stated quietly.

"No, I'm far sexier than the stuck-up angel who was sitting here before," a male voice answered.

Forty

"Thank you," Mel continued as if he'd neither spoken nor insulted Gabi. She took a bite and the piece came away bigger than she'd expected – certainly more than she could swallow. The swan stretched up eagerly to help her.

Hellspawn by her side or possible hellspawn at her feet – Mel chose to give her attention to the bright-beaked bird. Acutely aware of the demon watching from the bench beside her, she bowed her head to the swan's level.

"You really shouldn't do that. Those birds

will take your fingers off or worse if they get close to your face…"

A careful beak took the bread from her, close enough for her to kiss if Mel felt inclined to do so. Instead, she pulled away and covered her mouth as she laughed. Quickly, she placed another piece between her lips for the swan, which stretched for it. As he took the roll from her, she stroked the soft, dark down at his breast.

"I think this is the first time I've ever been insanely jealous of a bird," Luce said.

Mel laughed again. "There are more rolls, if you're hungry – Gabi said she'd bought plenty, though I'm not sure if she factored you into her numbers. I thought this little party was just for Lili's unit."

"Lili always invites the Executive to any unit meetings or functions – and it turned out that I was available to attend this one. Lucky me!"

Luce stretched an arm back to reach for another roll, splaying his legs out in what Mel hoped was simply an attempt to maintain his balance on the bench. His thigh pressed against hers as his shiny, shod foot nudged the swan.

The swan angrily lifted his wings a little, as if unsure whether to fly or fold them again. Luce leaned forward, a piece of bread extended toward the bird, and his feet landed heavily as his centre of gravity shifted. One shoe hit the grass, while the other found a webbed foot.

Wings unfolded fully, the swan hissed menacingly at Luce, before taking the food and a chunk of flesh from his hand. The ungainly bird waddled back to his little harem by the water's edge.

"Damned devil birds," Luce growled, swiping at his bleeding hand with a handkerchief as black as the blood seeping through his fingers. She'd never seen black blood before, but she tried not to stare. "I've seen drunk demons cause less trouble."

"He was well-behaved for me," Mel said. "If you hadn't stepped on his foot…Here, let me help." She reached for his injured hand, shifting the handkerchief away so she could see the damage. The small nick in the webbing between Luce's index finger and thumb looked too tiny to have bled so much. In fact, the skin didn't even look as if it had broken…She wiped away a little of the blood with the burgundy cotton in her hand to get a closer look.

The black handkerchief had turned dark red. Oh Hell, she thought.

Mel quickly released Luce, hoping he wouldn't realise what she'd done. She resolved to control herself better in future – changing the colours of demons' clothing while she healed them would only lead to trouble. She had to subdue her normal angelic instincts or risk exposing herself.

Too late – Luce fingered the red fabric thoughtfully before returning it to his pocket. "That doesn't mean the infernal bird isn't a demon – just that he's smart." Luce lowered his voice. "I'd lie down and be as docile as you desire for a piece of you, angel. Provided I get what I want from you in return…"

A chorus of honks was all the excuse Mel needed to turn her back on the dirty-minded demon, for she now had three hungry swans to contend with – the male and his two female friends. She filled three beaks with bread before she spoke. "I prefer to be called Mel, Luce. And just because a bird has black wings, doesn't make it a demon." She nodded at the male. "He's only a juvenile. His mother, though, has all her feathers." She offered another piece of bread to the female closest to him. Mel slid her hands down the bird's sides, causing her to open her wings and give them a few flaps before folding them again. The white feathers edging both wings stood out like the frill on the hem of Mel's skirt. "No demon or fallen angel has white feathers in their wings. All three are simply beautiful, magnificent birds. Let me show you."

Mel cupped Luce's limp left hand in hers. She could feel the darkness surrounding his soul far more strongly now, but she paid little heed to it. It didn't seem so dark…as if the thick layer of blackness was merely an illusion and the reality was more like the storm clouds she kept sensing. Clouds that parted at her delicate touch. Beneath, shrouded in shadow, there was so much she hadn't seen before.

Reaching for Luce's right hand, Mel placed the last piece of roll between his fingers. She extended his unresisting arm to tempt the swans with the bread. She could feel his fear. How could this demon be so terrified of a bird? "It's all right," Mel murmured, wrapping her own fingers around his so that she'd take the brunt of the swan's beak if it was startled. She felt Luce relax a little.

The larger female stepped forward to accept the offering and Mel brought Luce's empty hand to the bird's breast. She helped him stroke the dark feathers as she probed his soul.

It wasn't the bird that frightened him. He feared…pain. She dug deeper. Despair, darkness and disguised light, hiding behind…

The bird honked softly and ambled away.

"You're brave," Luce said, pulling his hands back as his voice darkened to an ominous depth. "You shouldn't have done that."

Mel heard the hollow echo in the empty threat and ignored it. Instead, she tried to hold on to the impression she'd felt, which slipped away faster than the swans waddling back to the water. She'd thought a demon's soul held nothing but darkness, yet she'd seen so much more. There was tenderness, too, and…something so slippery she couldn't grasp it, though she doubted Luce could yet, either.

"Brave? How?" she asked. "For showing you that the beauty of a bird is part and parcel of his black wings?"

"I don't think any other angel's tried to touch me without my permission before – and definitely no demon has. Afraid that with one touch, I could taint them. With a word, seduce them to surrender their souls to me. It wouldn't be the first time. You…you should know the risks you take. Believe the warnings and stories the older, more experienced angels tell you about me – chances are they'll all be true. You have the makings of a good angel, if you last long enough in the job. Isn't there an archangel in your unit? She knows who and what I am. She knows how best to protect herself, too. That one would probably walk away instead of having a conversation with me." He jerked his head at Gabi, who was grumpily crossing the grass a hundred metres away. "Don't you fear for your soul, Mel?"

She lifted her eyes to meet his, wondering if he knew how much she'd already read of his soul – and how much more he revealed to her in his dark eyes now. She smiled as she said, "Perhaps I have less to lose than the others. I rarely regret my actions and I don't now. It seemed sad that you would curse a creature for the colour of his wings – calling him a demon for defending himself. I've always loved the black swans here – for their contrast of darkness and light. Pure white wings can get very boring when that's all you see."

"I rarely see white wings at all." Luce didn't break her stare, letting her even deeper inside. "You really like swans, don't you?" If he was trying to read her soul, he'd soon learn that she had nothing to hide. Unlike him.

"Yes," she said simply. As she delved into his innermost soul, she found the need to continue. "Perhaps because I see more than most and it's hard to fear what you know so intimately. Darkness concealing light, at a depth where most won't look. A destiny that can't be stopped, only delayed. A desire for…vindication. A broken heart that wishes to be healed. A penchant for proof, but not destruction. A soul hidden deep within ice.

Yearning, yet a strong fear of pain. Loneliness and longing for…"

His mouth hung open and his eyes held something that looked like fear. Mel wondered what else the demon could possibly be afraid of – his soul was damned and his place in Hell was permanent. What had the power to frighten Lucifer so much that it could take his power of speech and leave him struggling to say something?

He swallowed a couple of times before he could croak out, "Mel…"

"We have salt and pepper!" announced Ana, holding up two china shakers. "Thanks to the café up the way."

"Thanks to her theft from the café," Gabi grumbled, slumping to the bench across from Mel.

Mel felt bereft as Luce yanked his hands from hers. She couldn't remember taking them – or had he given them freely? Regardless, by holding his hands and staring into his eyes she'd seen so much of his soul that she was stunned. Luce was no soulless demon – he was as complex as any angel, though the illusive shroud of darkness had seemed so thick. He was hiding so much sadness and pain, too…

"Mel. Mel!"

Mel lifted her eyes to Gabi's face, wiping her tears away. "Yes?"

"You should go help those boys bring the cooked meat back. We'll set things up here at the table," Gabi said. Her eyes flicked suspiciously to Luce before returning to Mel.

"Sure," Mel replied, getting up. She felt Luce's eyes following her to the barbeque, but she didn't acknowledge the attention. She had a job to do and it didn't involve comforting despairing demons — no matter how deep his soul.

Forty-one

"She said we were just going to the café to get drinks!" Gabi hissed in Mel's ear. "I grabbed a couple of bottles to take up to the register, paid for them, and the demon had vanished! I didn't see her until I got outside, when she told me she'd stolen the salt and pepper shakers while I had them distracted. She even congratulated me on being a decoy. I'm an accessory to theft. They won't let me back into Heaven and all because of that damn demon…"

Mel nodded and made sympathetic noises as

she tried to fork her lettuce into her mouth without getting salad dressing on her nose. Perhaps there was some trick to it that she simply didn't know? She glanced around the table — no, it seemed everyone struggled with the lettuce, too. Even Luce, whose eyes shifted quickly from her to his plate when her gaze settled on him.

Smothering a smile with another lettuce leaf, Mel eyed her steak, wondering if it was well-done enough not to bleed all over her plate.

"Cooked to perfection," Merih said, sticking a large piece of pink-hearted meat into his mouth.

"I wanted rare," Lili complained, lifting her well-browned beef to her lips with distaste.

"It is rare," Gerry chortled. "How often do you get a meal cooked by Merih and me? Merih even burned his hand making it. Now that's dedication!"

Merih held up his hand, which looked a little redder than usual.

"Oh, let me help you with that," Mel said, reaching for the demon's injured hand.

Gabi's loud laughter made Mel turn to the

angel in surprise. "Don't waste your time. Angels can't heal demons, Mel. You'd only burn him worse."

"Oh!" Mel remembered Melbourne Cup Day. "I'm sorry," she said to Merih. Yet she wondered how she'd managed to heal Luce, less than an hour before…

Mel decided her steak was worth the risk and cut herself a slice. It seemed demons weren't too bad at barbequing flesh. Perhaps it was all the practice they had in Hell.

"…and what will I do? We're angels. We're supposed to be perfect, not engage in petty theft on some lowly demon's demand!" Gabi hissed, her eyes filling with tears.

Mel carefully swallowed her morsel of meat. "Angels aren't perfect, Gabi. We're just good." She attempted to fold another piece of lettuce onto her fork, which flipped off just before she managed to insert it into her mouth, slapping her wetly on the nose.

"Not just good," Gabi insisted. "We're better than everyone else. At everything."

Mel laughed. "Better at stealing salt shakers, too?" she asked gently.

Gabi reddened.

"What's the joke, Mel?" Gerry asked, drawing her eyes away from Gabi. "It must be pretty good if it can make an angel blush."

Demonic laughter sounded on all sides.

Mel lowered her eyes. "It's…well, it's sort of a private angel joke. You probably wouldn't find it very funny. Even Gabi didn't like it – so I shouldn't really have said it in the first place."

"Tell us another one, then!" Merih insisted.

Mel smiled and shook her head. "I don't know many and the few I do know aren't very good. How about you tell one? I'm sure you know better ones than I do."

Merih grinned back. "Well, I do know a good one about the day Anna Nicole Smith and Princess Diana arrived at the gates of Heaven for judgement. Heaven was full and St Peter said they only had space for one more…"

"Why is he staring at you? He shouldn't be staring at you like that. It's so rude…" Gabi hissed in Mel's ear.

Mel turned to see who Gabi was glaring at. Luce averted his eyes again, so she looked back at Gabi.

"Um, you have mayonnaise on your nose, Mel," Gabi whispered, handing her a serviette.

Mel wiped her nose carefully, wondering how long she'd been wearing her lunch on her face. She hoped it had just been the last, floppy lettuce leaf that did it.

"…and St Peter said, 'Well, a royal flush beats a pair any day!'" Merih finished.

Mel laughed right along with the demons as Gabi grumbled about how judgement didn't work that way and Heaven was never full.

"I have one," Luce said. The whole table fell silent. He pulled out his red handkerchief and laid it on the table. He glanced up at Mel. "It's about a magic carpet."

"A man walks into a Persian rug shop and asks the salesman for the best rug he has. The salesman grins and tells him that his best rug is in fact a magic carpet. All he has to do is sit on the carpet and say, 'Magic carpet, rise,' and the carpet will rise and fly him wherever he wants to go. They bargain for a while, but when both feel they have a good price, they agree and the man goes home with his Persian rug/magic carpet."

Luce looked up at Mel expectantly before he continued, "So, the man lays the carpet on the floor of his living room, sits down on it and says, 'Magic carpet, please rise.' Nothing happens. He tries sitting in different positions, standing on it, shouting at it, cajoling it – all to no avail. The rug just sits there, looking pretty on the floor.

"The next day, he's having a beer with friends, and one's an engineer for an international airline. They get to talking and he asks the engineer for help with his magic carpet. The friend agrees and comes over to see what he can do for the carpet.

"The engineer takes one look at it and says, 'No wonder it won't fly. It doesn't have any wings!' and he gives it wings."

Mel leaned forward to see Luce fold the handkerchief, as if he was starting to construct a paper plane. She wondered how handkerchief planes flew.

"After his friend left, the man sat on his carpet again, saying, 'Magic carpet, please rise.' Still nothing. Annoyed, upset, but not ready to give up yet, the next day he decides to go ask a mechanic for help. So, he loads the carpet into the car, takes it to his mechanic and shows him the carpet.

"The mechanic looks at the carpet, the same way he looks at the man's car when it's going to cost a lot of money to fix, and finally says, 'Of course it can't fly. It doesn't have an engine!" So, the mechanic puts an engine on the carpet."

Luce folded the handkerchief again, tucking part of it underneath the rest, so it didn't look like a paper plane at all. He caught Mel's eye and winked. Intrigued, she crossed her arms and gave a slight nod, inviting him to continue.

"He pays the mechanic and takes his carpet home again. He lays it out on the floor, hops on, and says, 'Magic carpet, please rise.'" Luce paused for effect. "And…nothing. The carpet just sits there, looking like an ordinary Persian rug, with wings and an engine. Angry, he loads the carpet into his car, determined to take it back to the shop to get his money back.

"On his way back to the rug shop, he drives through the red light district, and the girls are out on the street, looking for customers. He has to stop at an intersection and a girl wearing not much at all leans into his open window, offering to cheer him up for a price.

"Feeling like it's the best thing that's happened to him all week, he agrees and he takes her back to his place. She notices the carpet and asks about it.

"He replies, 'It's supposed to be a magic carpet, but it doesn't matter what I do. It just won't rise!'

"The prostitute laughs and says, 'Baby, trust me, I can make anything rise.' So she gets her hands on the carpet and…"

Mel looked at the red origami penis rising in front of Luce and burst out laughing. The demons were strangely silent.

Luce gave Mel a cheeky grin. "Glad you like it."

The other demons took this as their cue that the joke was over and it was time to laugh, but Luce's eyes locked on Mel's and he seemed not to notice the others at all.

"I need a coffee," Gabi announced, shoving away from the table. The force of her push toppled Mel's wineglass over – right into her lap.

Gabi hunted around the table for a spare napkin to mop up the mess, but the napkins seemed to be gone. Mel rose and attempted to wring some of the wine out of her soaked skirt, hoping it wouldn't hurt the grass.

Luce stood, too, giving his ruddy penis a flick so it hung limp, an ordinary handkerchief once more, before holding it out to Mel. "Please," he offered.

Mel took the handkerchief, to the combined gasps of Gabi and the other demons, and used it to mop the moisture from her skirt.

Mel felt Gabi's hand close on her arm. Gabi was so agitated, her soul felt like a violently shaken snow globe: a blizzard of white with glimpses of colour. "Give it back," Gabi hissed, digging her nails in. "We'll go get napkins from the café."

Mel held out the well-used hanky, inclining her head to Luce. "Thank you."

He winked again. "Any time."

Gabi's grip tightened further as she almost dragged Mel away from Luce and the other demons, marching as fast as her legs could carry her. She looked close to tears. "That was Lucifer. The infernal Lord of Hell. In perhaps the sexiest body I've ever seen him in. And you…you took his dick and wiped your wet patches with it. Are you trying to tempt him to taint you? He's the most dangerous demon there is!"

"Relax. It was just a joke, Gabi, and it was a handkerchief, not the man's genitals. I'm hardly in danger from him," Mel tried to tell her, but Gabi seemed to be muttering under her breath, so she probably didn't hear.

Privately, Mel wondered what Gabi would say if she told her she'd touched more than Luce's suggestive handkerchief today. She didn't want the demon's body – she wanted his stormy soul.

"We should go back to the agency office. Raphael requisitioned a team of surveillance angels – Grigori – and those guys look like the best in the business. Living Greek statues, the lot of them, and they obey orders like you wouldn't believe. Tell Raphael you need one for the weekend. You take your pick of the

Grigori boys and…well, once you're done, that demon's hot body won't work on you. You should never go up against demons without making sure there's no desire for temptation…"

Mel burst out laughing. "Gabi, I'm not using any of the agency staff as sex toys."

Gabi looked hurt. "Not sex toys. A willing partner who'd do anything for you…"

"Gabi, have I ever told you about my friend, Patrick?" Mel asked carefully. She waited for Gabi's head-shake before she continued, "A few weeks ago, when I was in Colombo, I ran into him. I think I have a couple of photos we took on our wahoo cruise…"

Mel heard a clink and noticed the stolen salt and pepper shakers in Gabi's pocket. Gabi was certainly a conscientious angel today. Mel wondered how the barbeque would have ended had Gabi not been there.

Forty-two

She'd enjoyed the break over Christmas and New Year, but it looked like the peace was over. Protesters were camped out in front of Mel's office building again. Sighing, she slipped past them and wondered what the problem was this time. They looked like environmentalists – she could see very few shoes among any of them. There were plenty of placards and even one poor person in what looked like a black bird suit. Mel hoped he didn't get heatstroke in the hot weather that was forecast for the day – perhaps he'd head home before that happened.

She wished the security guard a good morning before she stepped into the lift. She could see him shaking his head at the strangely dressed protesters as the steel doors slid shut.

Reaching her desk, Mel flicked on the power to her PC and debated whether to take one of her tisane tea bags or if she'd need the buzz of a coffee.

Lili appeared. "Ah, Mel – you're needed over in Regulation. Zaq has some protesters causing trouble, so his report suddenly became a lot more urgent to the Minister. Something about cockies or corellas or kookaburras – ah, birds, anyway. Go find out what he needs done."

Mel nodded. "Sure." She set off in the vague direction Lili had waved toward. Her drink decision could wait until she worked out what her workload would be.

Thanks to the nameplate by his desk, Mel found Zaq, a stressed-looking demon who didn't even look up as she stood beside him.

She waited, watching him grit his teeth and tap the keyboard for almost a full minute before he grunted, "I'm busy. Go away."

Mel smiled. "I'm Mel and I'm here to help. I believe you have a protester problem?" She pulled out the visitor chair and perched on the edge of it.

"No, they're not a problem. They just don't like the airport expansion project we approved last week." He shoved a report at Mel.

Mel took the booklet and glanced at the cover. It wasn't the international airport – it was the one for small planes, not far south of her house. "I thought they were already so busy that the state government's trying to move them somewhere else," she said. "Why do they want more traffic?"

Zaq shook his head irritably. "They don't. They want to stop the traffic jams on the tarmac, waiting to take off. And then there are the flight schools…"

"There are flight schools there? I had no idea…" Mel marvelled.

"Sure. A couple of really big international airlines have their flight schools at Cockburn. Or they did. One of the accommodation blocks was lost in a bushfire last week."

"Oh, how awful! I hope no one was hurt."

"Only the guy cleaning the barbeque. He was looking for a hose and the only one in the courtyard belonged to the wastewater treatment system – the gardener occasionally used the water on the lawns. Anyway, it was curry night in the cafeteria two days before and the tank was pretty full, so he opened the tap. The septic tank was under a fair bit of pressure, so some of the air escaped and the hotplate was still on. The methane hit the flame and…well, the explosion took out half the accommodation block and the adjacent shower block. Left a big crater, too. The student was lucky – we think the sewage sludge saved him from the worst of the burns. They had to pump his stomach, though, because they think he swallowed some of it…" Zaq chortled. "That's when the shit really hit the fan. Turns out there were disused aviation fuel tanks under the dorms and maybe a plane or two, as well. The whole lot went up, just under the air conditioning units for the other accommodation block. Until they get the mess remediated – and best estimate is two or three years for that – they need new accommodation built quickly. The airline's insisting it can only go on land that the airport can guarantee isn't contaminated, which pretty much only leaves them the virgin bushland buffer. So those old trees have to go." He shrugged.

"Ah, so the protesters are upset about the loss of the trees?" Mel asked.

Zaq snorted. "Only because they think some endangered cockatoos need them. Someone should tell the protesters that any cockatoo in an airport is endangered until it's dead. Should've called it Cocky-burn Airport. It's the busiest airport in Australia – a quarter of a million takeoffs and landings every year. The cockies don't need the trees. The airport had experts come in to do surveys. They said it was too far north for the cockies, but they agreed to plant some trees to replace these, just in case someone got upset. So, no worries!"

Mel wet her lips. "So, what exactly is the Minister worried about, that he's putting you under so much pressure?"

"He needs a presentation that he can deliver to the press conference tomorrow, with briefing notes on the cockies. You know how to use PowerPoint?" Zaq eyed her critically.

"Sure," Mel replied, hoping he wasn't thinking about Luce's end-of-year presentation. "So all the info I need is in this report?"

"Yep," he said. "The expert reports are in the file on the network. I'll email you the link now. What's your login?"

Mel grimaced. "Melody Angel."

"That's a weird name for a…" He stopped. "Are you an agency girl?"

Mel nodded swiftly. "Yes, I'm from the Helpful Angels Agency."

Zaq's eyes narrowed. "Are you sure? You're not like the others. Even the boys in Legal…they have that 'I'm-better-than-you-and-I-know-it' air to them. You seem almost normal – like a human or something. I guess you haven't been an angel for long enough to get a trumpet up your arse or whatever makes them so stiff."

Mel laughed. "No, nothing musical in me at all. Just the name."

"And your voice," he said immediately, then

blushed. He stared into his lap as he continued, "So, can you get that presentation to me by the end of the day?"

"Sure," Mel said. She brandished the booklet. "Cockies, here I come!"

"I see why Lord...I mean, Luce recommended you," Zaq said.

Mel stopped dead, then proceeded cautiously with, "Lord Lucifer recommended me for this project? Why?"

"He said you were the best assistant he'd ever had for a presentation and to beg Lili to let me have you," Zaq mumbled to his lap.

Mel tried hard not to laugh. "You had to beg Lili for me? I bet she liked that."

Zaq laughed, lifting his head so he could look at Mel again. "Better you than her. Will you help me with the presentation? I'm terrible at them."

"Of course. Helping people is what angels do," she responded with one final smile, before turning to go.

Lord Lucifer, she mused. So it was true and Gabi was right. Luce was the Lord of Hell. She'd expected him to be darker inside, to be honest, but she only knew what she'd heard of the demon – Mel had never spoken to him before she'd set foot in the HELL Corporation offices. He just didn't seem as dangerous as Raphael and everyone else had warned her.

Ah, he was known as an expert in deception – perhaps he was capable of using that demonic deception on her, Mel decided.

She carried the report to her desk and swapped it for her mug. A tisane today – preparing a presentation on birds sounded like fun.

Forty-three

Mel was almost done with the presentation, which was full of pretty pictures of planes and the wildlife that did live at the airport, including some unusual orchids they seemed to be going to great lengths to protect. She couldn't work out how one of them could be called a praying virgin orchid – it looked more like a bird bending over to drink.

After checking the brief summary on the cockatoos in the report, Mel decided she needed more detail. She dug the expert's report out of her email and took a sip from her second cup of tea. It looked like he'd done a complete biological survey, counting birds, snakes, lizards and even moths.

Mel headed downstairs to pick up some lunch so she could eat while she read the lengthy report. She glanced at her phone and noticed the missed calls from earlier that morning. Raphael had some urgent issue again, she saw – three calls and a misspelled text message told her so. Alone in the lift, she dialled and held her phone to her ear.

Mel only waited for Persi's greeting before interrupting the girl to ask for Raphael. Persi's switchboard skills had improved – she managed to put the call through to Raphael on her first attempt.

"Why the barrage of messages?" Mel asked.

"Where are you? It sounds noisy. Can you come to the office this afternoon? I'd prefer not to be overheard," Raphael said.

"That's all? You want to see me? If you want privacy, come to my place. I'm cooking tonight – I'll make sure there's enough for you. I'll pick up fresh mushrooms on my way home for the risotto, if you bring some wine. I'll probably use all of mine in the cooking."

She stood in front of the Yummi sandwich shop and counted. As she expected, she didn't get past three before he said, "All right. What time?"

"Make it seven, just in case I get caught up at work," Mel replied. A Turkish bread caught her eye. Chicken, pumpkin, feta, baby spinach…her stomach rumbled its agreement.

Raphael agreed and they ended the call. Mel slipped her phone back into her pocket, caught the shop assistant's eye and claimed her sandwich. She waited while it toasted and carried the hot, papered bundle upstairs, her mouth watering all the way.

With every delicious bite, she learned more about the birds the biologist called forest red-tailed black cockatoos. He stated three times that the birds were native to the southern part of the state and rarely appeared on the Swan Coastal Plain, which Mel knew was where she stood. She paused in her reading to pop a few cockatoo facts into the presentation, including the expert's adamant statement that the birds didn't live, eat, sleep or breed at the airport.

She skimmed the rest of the report, hoping she'd see more pictures of the wildlife the eminent doctor and his team had encountered during their survey. She admired the pretty pictures of the tawny frogmouth and the legless lizard that looked like a snake, before opening to a large spread on cockatoos.

She was arrested by the detailed pictures of a small flock of the black birds. They seemed to hang effortlessly in the air, not a single one flapping its wings when the shot was taken. She counted them – nine, no, ten of the birds. Another shot showed the same birds soaring in front of a building that looked suspiciously like an airport control tower. She looked more closely – it definitely did look like the blocky tower at Cockburn. The caption beneath confirmed it.

So much for the cockatoos never coming to the airport. Perhaps they were holidaying – without eating, sleeping or breeding, she mused. The biologist dismissed them as an unusual occurrence – ten birds was hardly a viable population – and they'd never been seen before the 2009 survey. He considered it unlikely that they'd return, especially with the trees removed. They'd most likely move on to better places to feed, breed and whatever else they did in between.

Mel finished her lunch and her presentation before emailing the link to Zaq. She headed for his desk to ask if he needed any more assistance before she left for the day, and found him avidly reviewing her work.

He glanced up as she approached, but his eyes drifted back to the screen. "I love it! This is perfect," he gushed. "I know why Lord Lucifer's so in love with you. I'm more than halfway there myself. You're an absolute angel!"

Mel carefully kept her face blank as she considered his strange choice of words. Demons didn't – couldn't – love. It was against their very nature to do such a thing. Even the thought of a demon fancying himself in love with an angel was a crazy concept. Zaq must be more overworked than he appeared. "Well, that's what I am," she said.

"I owe you dinner. What are you doing tonight?" Zaq asked. His eyes shone with a fervour that Mel might have called lust, then amended it to excitement. He was staring at her face, after all, and not the rest of her body.

"I already have plans," Mel said gently. "I'm having dinner with a friend of mine tonight."

"Oh." The light in his eyes died, but then a tiny spark kindled again. "I still owe you one. If you ever need a favour, anything at all, just let me know. I'm your man." He grabbed her hand and kissed it.

Just like Luce – no sparks, no electricity.

The momentary contact was all Mel needed to see the man's soul – or the darkness surrounding it. His was a deep, velvety black – so dense she couldn't pierce the shroud at all. He may as well have had no soul, for all she could perceive. Yet the darkness seemed to be stretching, as if some tidal force dragged it toward her. Shaken, she pulled her hand out of his grasp.

Mel heard Zaq's mumbled apologies and thanks as he blushed profusely, but she was too lost in her own thoughts to do more than acknowledge him with a nod as she headed back to her desk.

She dropped into her chair and tried to sort through her findings in her head. The CEO was a demon, the Lord Lucifer she'd been warned about more times than she could count. But his soul and its demonic shroud were lighter and less dense than those of the demons he commanded. Was he a demon at all? How could the ruler of Hell be anything but a demon? And this talk of demons and love. That she knew to be impossible. Zaq's demonic soul-shroud had brooded with menace as she'd approached it for a closer look. Even the love in her soul had irritated it – love in a demon's soul would have the shroud attacking the soul it was supposed to protect. A cold soul, untouched by any outward emotion, locked in with itself. So lonely…was that why Luce had allowed her in?

HOW had Luce allowed her in?

The calendar on her computer trilled, telling her it was time to go home, so Mel shook the strange thoughts from her head and packed her bag to go. She powered down her computer, shouldered her bag and strode out. She needed to get this new information straight in her head before she shared it with Raphael. It wouldn't do to be uncertain — Raphael shied from risks, and letting her get this close to Luce looked like the biggest one he'd taken in a long time.

Time to catch the train, she reminded herself. Then get the best mushrooms and start dinner. Mushroom risotto was enough to make her night — and tonight she'd get to share the pleasure. What more could an angel ask for?

Forty-four

It never ceased to amaze Mel how the crowd on the train could disperse so quickly once they'd left the station. It was less than a hundred metres from the station platform to the other side of the road, yet a hundred people were reduced to two – and then, just one, as Mel's fellow passenger disappeared down a side street.

She crossed the tiny park, where a dozen residents seemed to be exercising their diminutive, yappy dogs and casting dirty looks at the family who were playing with their golden retriever. Perhaps it was because the retriever's size and bark dwarfed their precious pets into insignificance. Actually, the fat tabby cat regarding the animals warily from a nearby fence was bigger than most of them.

Mel stumbled over a pile of gumnuts in the grass, only just catching herself before she fell. It looked like someone had stripped the little marri tree of its nuts and just left them lying there. All the nuts looked strange, though, as if someone had shredded the flared end of them with a sharp pair of pliers.

A nut landed beside her foot, so mangled that only a shallow bowl was left of it. Mel looked up in time to see a large, black bird spread its wings and soar, kaa-raaking as it fanned out the bright red feathers in his tail. He settled in another tree a few metres away and selected a nut, delicately holding it in one claw as he attacked it with the sharp tool that was its beak.

Another raucous call sounded from the other side of the tree, but Mel couldn't see the second bird. She kept walking.

She paused to wait for traffic before

crossing the road to the tiny strip of local shops. A chorus of kaaa-raaks was all the warning she had before the birds skimmed over her, all ten…no, eleven of them, Mel counted. Solid red fans and striped red-and-yellow tail fans, marking them as both males and females. Six females. They rode the sea breeze erratically – some sideways, some so close to the road that a car almost hit one before it lazily flapped and rose above the ute's roof and roll bar.

Perhaps the biologist had miscounted the cockies or his photos hadn't captured the whole flock, Mel reasoned. She threaded through the parked cars to the grocer's, loaded a bag with their award-winning mushrooms – as proclaimed by the row of Royal Show ribbons pinned to the wall above the mushie fridge – and added a small box of shaved parmesan. With her arms full of food, Mel headed for the counter to pay for her purchases. After an exchange of money and pleasant words, Mel tucked her purchases into her canvas shopping bag and headed for the small supermarket next door.

She stopped at their display of garden and pet supplies, spread across two shelving units on either side of the doors. 'Your garden can never have enough sun,' proclaimed one sign, illustrated with a line drawing of the harsh summer sun beating down on a line of daisy-like flowers. Beneath it was a shelf stacked with bags of sunflower seeds.

Mel considered the sign for a moment, then gave in. It would be lovely to have the gold flowers adorning her garden bed along the fence – and she'd probably be in the house long enough to enjoy them. At least working in HELL had some compensations. She slung a bag of seeds over her arm and headed into the shop in search of rice and pine nuts.

Her arms weighed down by two well-matched shopping bags, Mel left the shopping centre for the trek up the hill to her house. The cockies looked like they'd preceded her – they were making a racket and dropping gumnuts from the tree on her neighbour's lawn when she unlocked her front door.

Dropping her food purchases on the kitchen bench, Mel hefted the bag of sunflower seeds and took it out to the backyard, placing it carefully on her little outdoor setting table. She'd scatter the seeds in the morning – tonight, she had dinner to prepare for herself and Raphael. She hoped he wouldn't forget the wine, for it looked like she barely had enough for the risotto and it didn't taste the same without it.

Placing her largest pan on the stove, she crossed to the stereo for a little cooking music. Beethoven today, she decided. The CD that started with his Ninth…Mel waited for the cellos to start before she headed back to the kitchen.

Humming along, she washed and sliced the mushrooms, then heated a little oil in the pan. She tipped what had to be a whole kilo of mushrooms onto the hot metal, stirring it distractedly with a spatula. It seemed like only yesterday that she'd first heard this played in Vienna. Ah, the quality from the CD simply wasn't the same, but that wasn't a reflection on the musicians – merely her old speakers. Perhaps she should get some new speakers and transfer the music to her phone or her laptop…

Mel switched the stove off and heard a strange sound that definitely wasn't Beethoven. She glanced out the kitchen window and saw far more black than should be in her backyard. Oh, no…

Forty-five

Sunflower seeds were everywhere, the plastic packaging ripped open by a combination of beak and talon. The birds were perched on her back fence, as well as on the backs of her garden chairs. One was waddling through the mess of seeds spread across her outdoor table. It keeked at her before picking up a seed and cracking it with its beak.

Mel stood on the back step, not entirely sure what to do. All eleven cockatoos had decided to come to her place and they evidently liked sunflower seeds. The female one on the table –

the one who looked smaller and lighter-coloured than the rest – keeked at her again and the female perched on her garden chair kaa-raaked in response. Mum and her baby, most likely, which would make the male eyeing her from the other garden chair Dad…

Of course they didn't breed or feed at the airport. They seemed to be doing it in her backyard and probably the bushland nearby.

Well, it's not as if she needed sunflowers, Mel decided. The red-tailed birds were a noisy and colourful addition to her garden – plus, they didn't need watering, what with the lake at the bottom of the hill. She resolved to sweep up the mess in the morning, when they were done, before she bought them some more seeds to entice them back.

Mel headed back inside and started on the rice. More oil, some spring onions, rice, wine and stock…Beethoven's Ninth gave way to his Fifth.

"That smells like Heaven," said a male voice. Mel smiled. Light fingers landed on her shoulder, followed by whisper-soft lips on her cheek. "Or maybe it's you."

"Good to see you, Raphael. Could you pass me that other carton of stock? I figure this'll be done in about fifteen minutes…" She pointed and he complied.

"I'll get some glasses and open the wine, then?" Raphael suggested, reaching for the cupboard above the bench and surveying the small selection of glassware. He didn't wait for an answer and Mel trusted his judgement.

Over the sizzle of the pan in her hands, Mel heard the sounds of bottle opening and liquid glugging into glass. Raphael passed her a glass of chilled white. "In honour of a job well done," he murmured, clinking his drink against hers before he took a mouthful.

Mel sipped cautiously, rolling the creamy blend around her mouth before swallowing. "I didn't think you had any of this left. Age has only improved it, too…" She took a larger sip. "The job's not over yet."

Raphael gulped down more wine, as if steeling himself for a painful task. "Your part in it's almost over."

"Oh?" Mel smiled as she tipped the mushrooms into the pan with her cooked rice.

The liquid hissed into steam as it hit the hot metal. She sprinkled pine nuts on top.

"Gabi told me about the picnic."

"There were sausages and salad, some lovely rolls that she bought and I shared with the swans, plus a few bottles of wine. The demons told dirty jokes and one of them scared her by stealing something. It was a HELL Corporation event. I could hardly invite you, Raphael." She kept her eyes on dinner as she stirred.

"She said there's no doubt. Their CEO is Lucifer. And she told me he wouldn't leave you alone – spent the whole time trying to charm you, while you encouraged him!" He sucked in a breath, trying to bring his voice down. "Please, Mel…we have to get you out of there quickly. If he's starting to take a personal interest in you, best you leave before he finds out anything about you."

Mel switched the stove off. "He's lonely, Raphael. Luce likes office girls and he's looking for someone willing to listen to him for more than five minutes. Yes, he evidently likes me. I listen because I want to hear what he has to say. Once you get past his brand of sleazy, he says a whole lot more than he should. What better way to find out what his plans are than to ask him and let him tell me in detail? You're making this out to be much harder and more dangerous than it really is." She pulled a serving spoon from the drawer and started dishing up.

"So you're saying someone less qualified than you could do this? If all he's after is a bit of friendly companionship, someone to smile and nod as he spills all his secrets…your job really is done." Raphael watched Mel sprinkle shredded parmesan on top of their dinner. He looked like he wanted to rip the bowl from under her hands, he seemed so eager.

Mel handed him his plate to hide her hesitation. "Maybe," she said finally. "They'd need a good memory and they'd need to be willing to get closer to him than most angels would. Up to and including sex, perhaps, if you want this wrapped up quickly. I don't know many angels who'd be willing to let Lucifer touch them, let alone make him think they like it…" She stopped at the sight of

Raphael's fierce grin. "Who do you have in mind?"

"Persi," he said. "She's not an angel yet, but she's looking for a way to prove herself so that she can be. She's not averse to using her body to get what she wants…remember that motorcycle gang she took on, whose leader was possessed by a demon?"

"I remember," Mel replied, hiding her smile. Persi had come out of that with a penchant for ink and some very creative tattoos. The girl had shown her, too – an ornate halo that only her suitors or a midwife would ever see, surrounded by a montage of kneeling men that spread across her thighs and seemed to be creeping up her back. The artwork reminded Mel of Luca Signorelli and she wouldn't have been surprised if Persi had given the tattoo artist pictures from Orvieto Cathedral to copy. The faces of the damned were decidedly modern, though – and Mel was certain she'd recognised a couple of the bikies amid the crush of flesh. From the little she knew of Luce, he'd probably appreciate the artwork more than most. Perhaps it would even remind him of home. "You're right, she wouldn't shrink away from touching Lucifer. Quite the opposite…"

Raphael smiled happily. "So you agree – Persi's perfect for this. All we have to do is find a place for her in the office, where she can get close to the CEO, and you can bow out safely. No worries!"

Mel almost choked on her first mouthful. Anything involving Persi was hardly without worry. She swallowed, recovered, and replied, "She's still very inexperienced and that puts her in far more danger than I am in her place. Luce might spot that and exploit it. I'd feel terrible, having to tell her mother that we'd thrown Persi into Hell as cannon fodder to protect me. Give me a few more weeks, Raphael, while you try to find somewhere to slip her into the corporation. And don't place her anywhere that needs switchboard skills. She can't transfer calls to save her life!"

Raphael nodded, his mouth full of food. Mel had never seen him eat anything so fast. "Okay. It'll take me that long to find a vacant place to put her forward for. Tell me if anyone's secretary or PA is going on holiday. That'd be the easiest way to get her in..." He shovelled another large forkful of risotto into his face.

Mel was barely a quarter of her way through her food when Raphael jumped up to take his empty bowl to the sink. "I'll get changed in your spare bedroom, if that's okay. Do you want me to help you wash up, or do you mind if I eat and run?" he asked.

"I can take care of the dishes this time," Mel replied. "Why, do you have a date?" She smiled, recognising his eager excitement.

Raphael turned red. "I have a meeting in Heaven and I thought I'd dress up for the occasion..." He gestured at the shirt he'd hung over Mel's lampshade — one of his sexier ones, she was sure of it.

"Sure. Pop your business clothes in the laundry basket — I'll take care of them when I do my next load of washing. I think I still have a couple of your shirts in the guest room, from the other times you've popped in on your way through to Heaven." She leaned forward and kissed his cheek. "Tell my brother I said hello and give him a kiss for me."

Raphael's cheeks flushed redder still as he beat a hasty retreat to Mel's guest room. Mel wondered how much longer it would take before Raphael and her brother admitted the truth – and who would be the one to tell her.

Forty-Six

I love Valentine's Day, thought Mel. It makes you think…

"I hate Valentine's Day," an annoyed voice began behind her. "Having to buy flowers and a present, this big commercial thing…and you know she expects it…"

"I'd like to make something for her for Valentine's Day, you know, kind of personal," another male voice replied.

"But would she like that?" the annoyed voice countered.

"Well, she'd have to say that, because she'd

sound really shallow if she didn't, but she really wants something bought…"

He laughed. "I like that I can just buy flowers and chocolates and things, it's so much easier. Have you tried to get a restaurant booking?"

Now both of them were laughing. "Valentine's Day and Chinese New Year in the same week? I'd never get a table! We'll be having dinner at home tonight. I hate going out for dinner on Valentine's Day, it's always so crowded, expensive and romantic. " He made romantic sound like the worst adjective of the three. Mel ducked her head to hide her smile.

"Yeah, mate, me too. Who wants to go out to dinner on Valentine's Day?"

Mel thought that she'd enjoy it, to be among so many happy couples, celebrating their love together. The atmosphere could be absolutely blissful. Still, she'd never be able to enjoy her meal, knowing that her table could have been occupied by another couple instead of her self-indulgent self, so tonight she planned to stay home, too. But first, they all had a full day's work to do before that could happen.

The train stopped and Mel turned, recognising the shirts the men wore, marking the men as employees of a consulting firm in the building across the road from the HELL Corporation. She couldn't recall what the company did – its logo featured the same mysterious combination of three letters that most such companies had. The crowd of commuters leaving the train soon separated her from the two anti-valentines and she exhaled her relief.

It was hot already, so she kept to the shaded walkways for her stroll to the office. Beneath the glass ceiling on the plaza, someone had hung red lanterns to celebrate the start of the Year of the Snake. Below the lanterns, a florist had placed a huge display of red roses. "Only $99, a dozen roses delivered to YOUR Valentine!" said the sign painted on the window.

Mel walked past the florist. Something smelled beautiful and it sure wasn't the phalanx of red flowers. She entered the shop and the scent mystery was solved. She waited patiently for service from the angry florist and her stressed assistant.

"Why did you order so many Asiatics? No one wants Asiatics for Valentine's Day — everyone wants red roses! Now we won't have space in the fridge for what we really need!" The florist's face was growing as red as the flowers she was shoving into the refrigerator. "And chocolates — how could you order gold hearts when everyone wants red? We'll never sell these and they'll melt out of the fridge in this heat!"

The assistant looked about fifteen and ready to cry. "I didn't…you told me…" She proffered an order pad, pointing at handwriting that looked too old to be hers. "What do I do with the liliums?"

"Put them out on sale! If we can't sell them at four o'clock to the desperate men who forgot to order roses, you can throw them in the bin!"

Mel stepped up to the counter. "How much for the liliums?" The smell of them was tantalising. It had been so long since she'd had any.

The assistant looked at the florist, who didn't deign to reply. "O-on sssale today. Twenty dollars a bunch."

Mel smiled. "How about those chocolates?"

"Cost price plus GST," the florist said, her eyes showing her eagerness. "Thirty-three dollars."

Mel held out her Visa card. "Can you make up a large bunch of three of these, along with the chocolates, please?"

"Yes, ma'am," the assistant replied, trying to hide her smile from the florist as she made Mel's flowers as pretty as possible with pink paper and ribbon.

Five minutes later, her nose buried in the unearthly scent of her enormous bunch of liliums, Mel carried her flowers and chocolates into the office.

"Wow," said Lili as Mel passed her. "Who are they from?"

"An admirer," Mel replied. An admirer of Asiatic liliums who couldn't walk past them, she thought but didn't say.

Forty-Seven

Mel placed her flowers in a vase on her desk by the window, where she could smell and admire them all day. She took a pair of scissors to the large box of chocolates, so they were easy to reach in their display tub.

This was her favourite part.

"Good morning, happy Valentine's Day!" she sang out, handing chocolates to all of her colleagues, or placing them on the keyboards and mouse mats of those staff who weren't in yet. "Happy Valentine's Day…"

"Thank you," said Lili, looking stunned.

"This is the only Valentine's present I've had in years."

"Thank you," said Merih.

"Happy Valentine's Day!" replied Gerry.

"OH!" gasped Nybbas, turning red as he lost his ability for coherent speech.

Mephi smiled at Mel – the first such smile Mel had seen. "That's really lovely of you, dear. My husband doesn't even know what day it is."

Mel's smile wobbled with sympathy. What kind of life would it be, to live as a demon without love? She could barely imagine it. Wavering, she debated whether to give chocolate to the CEO, too. No one could be as lonely as Luce, the head demon himself, lusty looks and all. Perhaps she could just leave it with Mephi or on his desk. "Can you tell me if Luce is in?" Mel asked, peeking into the demon's office.

"He's at a meeting, but he'll be back shortly. Why? Did you want to see him about something, dear?" Mephi asked. "If you do, I'll be happy to slip you into his schedule. Just let me know and I'll arrange it." She winked.

"Ah, no, but thank you," Mel said quickly. "I

just thought I should leave him a chocolate, too. In the interest of fairness…" She hurried to his desk, placed the gold heart on his mouse mat, then escaped before he returned.

With a considerably lighter tub of chocolates, Mel returned to her desk. She unwrapped one of the gold foil hearts for herself. It wasn't like the foil colour made a difference to the taste, she thought, as the high-quality chocolate hit her tongue. She decided to have another one.

Gabi bounced into Mel's office. Mortified at missing her fellow angel from Reception, Mel offered the girl her pick of the chocolates. Gabi took several with a smile of thanks as she announced, "You have a delivery!"

Behind her, a courier struggled under an awkward armload of boxes. "Melody Angel?"

Mel cringed inwardly at her full name, but smiled and nodded. "That's me."

He carefully laid the boxes on the meeting table in the middle of the office. Heads rose above partitions, meerkat-style, turning toward her. "Sign here?"

Mel signed his electronic pad with one hand,

reaching for a chocolate with the other. She handed them both to him. "Thank you."

He looked surprised.

Mel smiled. "Happy Valentine's Day. Call it a small thank you."

The courier left, looking somewhat bemused.

"Go on, open them!" Gabi urged, her eyes shining.

Mel cut the ribbon on the first long box. A dozen long-stemmed roses lay nestled in tissue paper, topped by red ribbon and a card. "From a secret admirer," the card read.

The other two boxes contained identical displays, only differing in the handwriting on the cards. Mel leaned over the boxes in hope, but she was disappointed. The long-stemmed roses didn't smell. What was the point of giving roses anymore? Florists' roses didn't smell. It was the scent in the oil that was an aphrodisiac. Mel sighed as she remembered receiving scented roses. It seemed so long ago…wait, no it wasn't. There was that rose from the mysterious, disappearing stranger. The mature, red, thorny one that had made her think about…

"So are you my Valentine?" Luce asked with a grin, appearing out of nowhere with a gold heart between his fingers.

Mel's heart sank. She'd so hoped not to see him, watching his eyes wander as he said his insincere thanks. Too late now.

"Mel's wonderful," Gabi gushed. "She brought chocolates for the whole office to share and she's been delivering them to everyone. So sweet of her!" Mel held her breath as Gabi held out her handful of hearts, making Luce's single one seem insignificant.

Lili stuck her head in the office. "Thanks again, Mel!" She shoved her chocolate between her teeth as she withdrew.

For the first time, Luce looked stunned. Mel wasn't sure if she wanted to laugh or cry at the demon's expression. He'd come in with such self-confidence and now he was crushed.

"I wasn't sure if I'd have enough for everyone, so I only gave people one each," Mel said quietly. "I'd be happy to give you more, if you'd like." She started to smile again. "But only if you don't tell everyone else. I'm not sure if I have enough for everyone to grab a whole handful like Gabi did."

Gabi stuck her tongue out, then unwrapped a chocolate and popped it into her mouth.

Luce's dark eyes stared at Mel as he held up his heart. "This is the first gift I've ever received for Valentine's Day. Thank you." His expression was all seriousness – but he appeared sincere for once, Mel thought.

"You're welcome," she said with equal sincerity. She let her lips lift in a slight smile as Luce's scrutiny continued. A lesser angel might have looked away, but Mel was more than a match for poor, lonely Luce. She felt her sense of pity awaken.

He glanced away.

"Whose are those?" Luce asked, nodding at the boxed flowers.

Gabi swallowed her chocolate with a gulp. "Mel's!" she said, appearing more excited than Mel.

"Really?" Luce asked, looking Mel up and down. "You're a popular lady!" He hurried away without another word.

Forty-eight

"More for you, Mel!" Gabi sang out an hour later, interrupting Mel's lunchtime reading. She was quite growing to like the book about nephilim – the heroine reminded her strongly of Persi, with her penchant for shoes. She wondered if it was a distinctly nephilim quality or simply one Persi didn't share with the angelic half of her family heritage.

This time, Gabi held a large display box of orchids, in shades of fuchsia, gold and white. Mel picked up the card. "For my office angel, with compliments from a secret admirer," she read. She recognised Luce's handwriting, for his not-complimentary written rant was still clear in her mind.

Gabi didn't seem to want to leave. "Ohhhh, I love orchids," she cooed over the flowers. "Who sent you such beautiful ones?"

Mel caught sight of Luce, watching her avidly from a nearby cubicle. She turned her eyes to the flowers. "They're really lovely," she admitted. She leaned over to sniff these, too, but she could feel the chill in the petals as soon as she got close. Fresh from a florist's fridge, these wouldn't smell until they warmed a little. Disappointed, she just smiled at Gabi before going back to her project. She lost herself in looking for graphics for the unit's new phone app.

By the end of the day, Mel had moved both the orchids and the roses in their vases to the middle of the meeting table, where the whole office could admire the display. Only the liliums remained in the vase on her desk, still wrapped in paper, waiting for her to carry them home.

Her computer clock ticked over to knockoff time, so she shut it down and rose. She stared at the orchids for a moment, wondering whether to take them. Gabi liked them so much – she didn't want to deprive the girl of her favourite flowers. She bent and inhaled deeply, hoping to catch the scent of them to help her decide.

Nothing. The strongest smell came from the greenery surrounding the flowers.

With a sigh, she straightened again. They were so pretty, which almost made up for the lack of smell. Still, it would be near impossible to manage the box of orchids and the bunch of liliums on the train – and there was no way she was leaving her liliums behind.

She gathered her things and turned to go, her arms full of marbled pink and white blooms.

"Don't forget your flowers," Luce said, striding into the office. "You might drive one of your Valentines to despair by leaving his gift behind."

Mel smiled. "They're all from secret admirers. I thought we could all admire them here. Maybe having them on display will give some of the admirers the courage to admit who they are." Her eyes met Luce's and she knew the others would never say, for fear of his reaction. Poor Nybbas, Merih and Zaq. "I'll have my hands full on the train, anyway." She lifted her liliums up, so the divine scent wafted through the office again.

"I could give you a lift home, if you like, and help you carry all of these down to my car," Luce offered eagerly. "We could go out for dinner afterwards. I know this wonderful seafood restaurant, right on the water, which does the best oysters…"

"No, thank you," she said, edging past him. The last thing she needed was a demon – especially this demon – knowing her home address.

"Come on, Mel, you won't get a better offer than The Old Brewery. Fresh oysters, wagyu beef cooked to perfection, marron…the beautiful view over Melville Water as the sun sets…and you'll be with me." His grin widened with each new temptation, as if he felt he was saving the best for last. Mel was sure that, in his opinion, this was the case.

"Actually, I have plans for dinner already," she admitted.

"Who with?" he asked. He may as well have asked for the details of a serial killer who needed to be put away for life, Mel thought, not liking his tone.

"With the person who bought my liliums," she said gently.

"The cheapest flowers the florist had," Luce scoffed. "You can do better than him. Stand him up – come out with me instead. I promise you'll enjoy it."

"The flowers with the most alluring scent that the florist had, making them more than just beautiful," Mel corrected. "From someone who knows they're my favourite because of their perfume. Someone who didn't need to hide behind the anonymous name of Valentine or admirer." She looked Luce firmly in the eye. "Good night, Luce. I hope you enjoy your evening and your oysters. See you at work tomorrow."

She strode out, not slowing her step until it had carried her into the train carriage and the doors slid shut behind her.

A kind man offered Mel his seat and she took it gratefully, balancing the flowers between her knees. She held her phone out and looked for a short story to help her pass the time on the train, having finished the nephilim book at lunch.

While she searched, she heard a familiar voice.

"So, did you get her present?" the annoyed anti-Valentine of the morning enquired.

"Yep, flowers, chocolates and some earrings," replied the other. "We're going out to dinner tonight, at that new teppanyaki grill at Nishi. You?"

"My missus booked us into Beethoven's, for their special Valentine's banquet," the now-more-stunned-than-annoyed voice replied. "Have you ever been there?"

"No, but I've heard it's good. Have fun, mate!"

Mel hid her smile behind her flowers. The two men who wouldn't go to restaurants had booked dinner at two of the more expensive establishments in the area, but she knew from experience that the prices at both were certainly worth it.

She found a short story competition with a Valentine's Day theme and settled in to read some of the entries. Romance, unusual gifts and her favourite day of the year, with flowers and chocolate to scintillate her senses as she forgot all about Luce and his devious demands.

She happily headed home, ordered a pizza and opened a bottle of wine to share with herself. Amid the scent of her favourite flowers, she thought of Luce, dining alone amid a multitude of couples, lonely with his oysters by the river. Once again, she pitied the demon and anyone else who couldn't enjoy a day that was about love – whoever you spent it with. Perhaps she should have joined him. He would have spent the whole time ogling her and missing out on the lovely atmosphere places only had on Valentine's Day.

Poor Luce. It must be so sad to be a demon on days like this.

Forty-nine

Mel felt self-conscious as she stepped into the office. On the train, she'd been talking to a particularly talented artist who'd admitted to painting pictures inspired by the books she'd read and the discussion had turned to mermaids. What Mel hadn't said was that she knew for a fact that mermaids existed – and she'd met some. She and the demons could pass as humans among humans, but with mermaids it was a completely different story.

She dropped her bag on her desk, glancing at the big south window. Her computer was already on, which seemed strange.

"Good morning!" boomed a voice behind her. "What are you looking for?"

Spinning on the spot, Mel came face to face with a man she'd never met before. "I'm looking for my coffee cup, so I can have some caffeine before I check my emails," she replied uncertainly.

"Oh, were you the girl who borrowed my desk while I was away? I had your clutter moved to the desk by the fire escape, where it belongs." He dismissed her with a wave of his hand. "Try looking over there." He enthroned himself on what had been Mel's desk chair and ignored her as he placed his hand possessively over her former mouse.

Mel summoned a smile. "Thank you," she said as she left the bright shared office to return to the cramped, dark desk by the fire escape.

Gabi was waiting for her with a box full of Mel's belongings, the box of orchids balanced precariously on top. As soon as she saw Mel, her expression turned from bewildered to sad. "Mel, some new man told me I had to pack up all your things and move them. I didn't know what else to do – you weren't here and neither was Lili…"

Mel was calm and collected. As temporary staff, even her desk was only a temporary arrangement. Today, she wouldn't have to worry about showing off her stockings to everyone on the plaza. She could wear skirts as short as she pleased. "No worries, Gabi. It was too bright by the big south window and the air conditioning couldn't cope with the sun coming in on hot days. Thanks for taking such good care of my things. Now, if the rumours I heard downstairs on my way in are correct, we're very well placed for…"

The fire alarm began to sound over the office PA system. Gabi's eyes widened. The beeping lengthened to whooping as Mel smiled. They were the first to evacuate via the fire escape stairs.

Standing in Central Park as all the other staff meandered in, Gabi said, "You'll have to take your angel orchids home. They won't survive without some sun."

Mel shrugged. "Cut flowers never last long,

anyway. They were lovely while they lasted – much longer than the roses, at least."

Gabi's eyes grew round. "Your angel orchids aren't cut flowers. They're in a beautiful pot, with soil and everything. I've been watering them for you every week – it was the least I could do, in exchange for you sharing them with me. It was heavy, but I couldn't just leave them there!"

Live orchids. Luce had bought her a large pot of live…had she said angel orchids? "I've never taken care of orchids before," Mel admitted. "Aren't they meant to be really delicate? What kind are they? I'll have to look up detailed instructions on keeping them alive. I'd hate to kill them."

"They're moth orchids – but yours are a really rare angel colour-morph. I've only seen angel ones in fuchsia and pink, but yours are white with tinted lips and a delicate blush…it must be someone who knows you really well. And he must really like you – those are insanely expensive. Do you think it might have been one of the Grigori boys from the agency? I went down to watch them play football one lunchtime and they were the no-shirts side…" She blushed. "Well, if it weren't for Uri, I'd seriously consider a bit of fun with one of them. Those boys are built!"

Mel laughed. "No, I don't think they're from one of the agency angels, however well-built they might be. Wishful thinking, I'm sure – I don't blush anywhere near as much as you do."

"You should keep them in your bathroom, so you can admire them when you're all steamy in the shower," Gabi continued dreamily.

"What? The shirtless Grigori football team?" Mel tried to control her laughter. "They wouldn't fit in my tiny bathroom."

"No, your orchids. They like it warm and humid. I bet the guy who gave them to you would love to know his flowers share your shower every morning…"

Mel shook her head. "How long since you've seen Uri? Did you leave him in Russia?"

Gabi nodded sadly. "I haven't seen him in months. What with the next winter Olympics in Russia, he's worried and trying to keep an eye on everything. But I know I'll see him again eventually. It's you I'm worried about.

How long since you've seen a man in all his naked glory?"

Mel opened her mouth to reply.

"Good to see you ladies made it out unscathed," Luce's voice came from behind her. He nodded to Mel and Gabi as he breezed past, grinning. "Don't forget the Minister's visit later on this morning!"

Neither of them were likely to have any contact with the Minister – temporary staff were hardly going to be high on his list of people in the corporation to meet on his much-touted tour of the facility. Mel and Gabi didn't respond, letting Luce continue walking until he was out of earshot.

Hoping he hadn't heard their conversation, Mel's thoughts drifted to Luce's flowers and his Valentine dinner invitation. Perhaps she should have accepted, after all. The orchids had been a very kind gesture – more thoughtful than she'd given him credit for.

"See? I knew you couldn't remember," Gabi said. "Next time you're up at the agency, wink at one of the Grigori boys and take him home for the weekend. Share a shower with a man instead of just his flowers. I guarantee you'll be glowing come Monday morning."

She might do dinner with Luce, Mel decided, but sharing a shower with the demon? Hell, no! When this assignment was over, she'd socialise a little with the other agency angels and see what came of it, that's all. Or perhaps even pay Patrick a visit…

The red-hatted fire warden demons were signalling the all-clear, so Mel and Gabi started to move back to the office. The foyer was full of demons and humans, for there were still a few humans in the offices on the other floors. The lifts were leaving, packed with people.

"Mel," a voice hissed.

She saw a beckoning hand and followed it around the corner to the service lift, where an elderly security guard stood, smiling. "Care for a lift, Mel?"

She laughed and accepted, thanking him. Reaching her floor, she steeled herself for another day at work. Sitting next to the fire escape did have its benefits, even without a window, Mel mused.

Fifty

Thanks to the quick-thinking security guard, Mel was one of the first people to return to the office after the fire and evacuation drill. That meant no queue for the coffee machine. Mel dug her mug out in readiness for the luxury of a real coffee while her computer started.

The milk stood in crates by the fridge, cascades of condensation dripping down the sides of the bottles, while a new box of coffee beans sat unopened by the machine. The delivery must have arrived just as the fire alarm sounded, so Mel decided to take advantage of the surplus to serve herself precisely what she wanted. She selected a double with a little extra froth to fill her mug, and watched the drink make itself.

Mel carried the steaming concoction back to her desk and set it down so she could start unpacking her belongings.

The orchids were first. She looked around for a suitable spot where they might get a little sun and still be out of her way. Mel temporarily settled for the top of her filing cabinet, swearing she'd take them home on the train that night — they didn't deserve to die on her dingy desk, displaced by the demon from their accustomed window.

Pens and papers were much easier to place — two minutes saw everything in order once more. Mel sat to start work. She took her first sip of coffee as she checked her emails.

The girl she'd been talking to earlier that morning had sent a link to some of her recent character artwork, the first email told Mel. Mel clicked on the link and waited patiently for the gallery to load.

"Here's my little angel! Minister, I'd like you

to meet Mel, our miracle worker in averting alien invasions!" Luce's beaming face was the first thing Mel saw, with another be-suited man behind him.

Trying not to grit her teeth as she smiled, Mel stood and offered her hand to the newcomer, recognising the Minister for Productivity. He was the man who'd decided to start selling off government services, so the government of the day could fill what seemed to be a whole galaxy of budget black holes. Mel had always wondered whether giving government services to the Pit had been such a wise decision, but she'd never had the opportunity to ask the Minister his thoughts on the matter. Now was her chance.

She opened her mouth, trying to arrange the question carefully so she'd receive an answer.

"Wow! Isn't she a beauty?" the Minister exclaimed with a smile.

She closed her mouth quickly, wondering if the man was Luce's brother. Or his son. Or some close, salacious relation who Luce had trained in…

"You are a talented lady, aren't you, Mel?

When did you paint that?" Luce asked, his eyes intent on Mel's monitor.

"I'd like a copy on the wall in my office!" the Minister declared.

"Oh, no, my friend did it. She just sent me a photo so I could see…" Mel trailed off, unsure how to introduce the subject of mermaid fact and fiction with a minister.

Both Luce and the Minister started walking away.

Mel sank gratefully into her chair, watching to make sure neither man was looking to return. Her computer had blacked out to her screensaver, so she nudged the mouse to wake it up. She almost spat out her coffee.

A beautiful blonde mermaid, her breasts on full display in glorious colours, beamed from Mel's screen. She was, indeed, a beauty.

Never. She'd never agree to go to dinner with Luce, and she hoped never to lock eyes with the demon again. He'd seen naked mermaid pictures on her PC.

Mel felt her cheeks go well past pink, approaching the colour of those clearly visible nipples. "Oh Hell," she whimpered.

Fifty-one

"Another report for Luce?" Mephi asked, glancing up from her magazine.

Mel nodded. "Yes. This one's on cemetery sustainability. Who'd have thought cremation was more environmentally friendly than burial? Not to mention cheaper in the long term. It's all there – along with the economic assessment. I have a lot of pictures from my facility tour, but I didn't put them all in. The crematorium waste looked like something you'd scrape out of a baking pan after making a pork roast with plenty of crackling…" She saw Mephi's face turn white and then pale green as she set what looked like barbeque pork and fried rice down on the desk. "Sorry. It surprised me, is all."

Mephi coughed and wiped her mouth with a tissue. "It sounds…fascinating. You can take it straight in to Luce's office – pop it on top of the pile in his in-tray. Do you want me to schedule an appointment with him so you can discuss it? I can squeeze you in any time this week, as long as you don't tell anyone else I did it. He'll be back from his meeting with the Minister in an hour or two."

"No, the whole thing's pretty self-explanatory. If he wants to know any more, we can always arrange a meeting later," Mel said, moving to deposit her report on Luce's desk. As she returned, she caught sight of what Mephi was reading. It wasn't a magazine at all – it was a travel brochure for Thailand. "Are you headed off on holiday?"

Mephi looked uncertain as she set the brochure down. "Part of the arrangements for working here include paid holiday leave for all staff. I've never taken a holiday before and I wanted to spend the time at a spa resort somewhere, where it's warm and I can just relax."

"You've never..." Mel's sympathy for demons flared up. "Thailand is lovely. So's Malaysia, and Singapore, and Indonesia...or there's Mauritius...and Sri Lanka."

"But my husband wants to go skiing – he wants to see snow and spend his time somewhere cold before he heads back to...where he normally works," Mephi wailed.

"Snow can be wonderful, too," Mel said. "Very pretty – and the ski resorts usually have lots of warm food, well-heated rooms and plenty to drink."

Mephi looked stricken. "He said that he'll go without me if I won't go to a ski resort, and he refuses to go anywhere near the tropics. Too hot for him, he said. We've never been on a holiday together and I was so hoping..." The demon looked close to tears.

"You could do both," Mel suggested.

"He can't stand the heat," Mephi replied sorrowfully.

Mel hesitated for a moment, then took pity

on the demon. "How about a ski resort with hot spring spas? That way, he could ski while you relax, and in the evenings, perhaps you could share the spa..." She winked. "The hot water certainly gets the blood flowing, I've heard."

Mephi stared at her. "What would an angel know about...about..." She blushed.

Mel laughed easily. "My friend, Koyane, lives in Japan. When I visited him in '97, we spent some time in the hot springs around Kyoto and Nara and they proved quite steamy. I had some spare time, so he took me up to the Nagano region and showed me some of the natural hot springs, outside in the snow. There was this one little town...Nozawa Onsen, it's called. It's a ski resort, but it's named for the sulphur spring onsens. Between the apple ice wine, the hot springs, the snow and Koyane...well, I wasn't in a hurry to come home."

"Bob would like that, if there's skiing, and if there's some sort of spa for me..." Mephi looked wistful. "Is there anywhere you can recommend for us to stay?"

"Sure. There was this lovely traditional guesthouse, owned by a Japanese lady I met in an onsen. I was feeling ill because I'd had far too many shiitake with my soba…ah, you don't need to hear about that. Anyway, I can email the details of the place, if you like, and you and Bob can make your trip something of a second honeymoon. In the traditional guesthouses, the beds are all futons on tatami – wall-to-wall mattresses. More space than the average couple know what to do with. The honeymoon suites with their king-sized beds here don't know what they're missing…"

"It sounds wonderful," Mephi admitted. "Four weeks there sounds almost as good as going back to Heaven…"

"Oh – have you and…ah, Bob been together for that long?" Mel asked, trying to hide her surprise.

Mephi nodded. "We met before the battle and we sort of got together before the fighting started…" She blushed again. "When Lucifer fell, we refused to be parted and we weren't allowed back in." She sighed. "It was a long time ago and the fires then have sort of burned down to a dull glow, but I still remember what that first night was like. I'd give almost anything to have that again with Bob."

Mel couldn't hide the tears that sprang to her eyes. Demons who still had the memory of a love that preceded their fall. Admittedly, it could hardly be more than lust now, but even that was something, after all this time. Who'd have thought that Mephistopheles and Beelzebub were even capable of love in the first place? Maybe there was hope for them, after all. "I'll go get their contact details and send them to you straight away," Mel promised and hurried away. First, she'd find the details of that ryokan for Mephi. Then, she'd call Raphael and tell him she had the perfect job for Persi – as Luce's PA. Serendipity, indeed.

Fifty-two

"It's time for you to finish up in the office. Book your flights to Korea whenever you're ready. Persi got the job and she can clean up the last details," Raphael announced, rummaging through her cupboards. "Where do you keep your coffee?"

"I don't have any," Mel replied absently. "I drink more than enough at the office. What makes you think it's over?"

Raphael stared out the window, which Mel thought was definitely suspicious. "You've said Lucifer is looking for some female company.

Persi's more than willing – she'll start as soon as his PA leaves the office. You can mentor her for a week or so, but it's time to pull you out of there before it gets too dangerous."

Mel snorted with laughter. "The office is dangerous? Raphael, they're just demons. I can handle myself just fine."

He whirled and met her eyes. "They're not just demons. It's an office full of demons led by Lucifer. Do you know how dangerous he can be? And he's paying a lot of attention to you – you've said it yourself." His fingers plucked nervously at his tie. Mel had never seen the man look so unsettled.

"I've managed to keep him at arm's length for this long, Raphael. I'd prefer to see this through personally, or I'll be worrying the whole time I'm in Korea. Persi isn't all that experienced and you don't seem to be so worried about Luce getting his hands on her."

"Please, Mel. None of us wants to see you in Hell – get out while you can. Let Persi finish this up, so you can stay safe."

Mel shook her head. "I still don't see how sacrificing Persi for my safety is acceptable.

She's unpredictable and inexperienced, but she might make a good angel if she gets the chance. Sending her in as cannon fodder for Luce is a waste."

Raphael managed a weak grin. "She said the same thing – about wanting a chance. And this is it. I'm giving her a chance to prove she deserves to be an angel. It's what she wants, she said."

"I don't think…" Mel hesitated, then began again. "I realise she's eager to prove herself, but this is a Hell of a responsibility for someone like her. Even if I'm not in the office, I'm not leaving for Korea before her task is complete. I want you to make it clear that she's to call me if she has any news – good or bad – and if she needs even the slightest bit of help. Day or night. And I will be watching her, because I don't trust Lucifer."

Inwardly, she sighed. She still wanted his soul, but she'd have to wait and give Persephone her chance first. Luckily, she had eternity.

Fifty—three

Mel took a bite of her sandwich. Time for lunch, she thought, wondering if she'd have time to start reading that story about a grumpy unicorn and a gunslinger. Mermaids might exist, but unicorns were definitely the stuff of fiction. Romancing a rhinoceros, really. Or like passing Persi off as an angel. Add a rider and… She pulled out her phone and started looking through her library.

"Ah, Mel?" Lili's head popped up over the partition. "You're not busy tonight, are you? There's a big executive meeting last thing this afternoon, to fit with the CEO's schedule, and Mephi's gone on leave. Could you stay to take the meeting minutes and write them up afterwards?"

Mel looked up from her phone. "Shouldn't it be one of the usual admin people in Executive, who know more about confidential, high-level stuff?"

Lili looked abashed. "Well, yes, but Mephi recommended you to Luce and he requested your services, so…"

Mel felt her lips curl in a customary smile. "Of course. I don't have plans tonight after work." Except eating dinner, she thought but kept to herself. "I'd be happy to help out. Does that mean I'll get time off in lieu of the extra hours, or do you just want me to put the hours on my timesheet as overtime?"

Lili shrugged. "Your call. I don't mind. Can you ring Mephi to tell her you'll do it?"

"Isn't Mephi away?" Mel asked, mystified.

"Yes, but there's some temp doing her job until she comes back. She'll be at Mephi's desk." Lili dismissed her and disappeared.

Mel picked up the phone and dialled

Mephi's extension.

"Hello, HELL Corporation Executive. This is Persephone. How may I direct your call?" The breathless voice sounded like a child's. Mel envisaged pink, bubble gum and knee socks, carefully camouflaging what she knew to be a very naughty tattoo, framed in black lace. If Persi remembered to wear underwear at all, Mel mused, recalling one incident in the US where Persi had refused to wear something Americans called panties, to the delight of the media crew. She hoped Persi could do a better job this time. This was too delicate a task to leave details hanging in the wind.

Mel took a deep breath. "Persi? It's Mel. Just calling to say I'll be taking the minutes at the executive meeting this afternoon."

"Oh!" Persi squeaked, giggling. "I'm so nervous! I've never had so much responsibility – personal assistant to a CEO and all. He's so attractive, too…"

Mel smothered a smile. "Sounds like you're doing fine, Persi. Can you tell Luce for me, please?"

"Oh…oh, sure!" Persi bubbled. "One

second…sir! Miss Angel has confirmed that she will be available to attend the executive meeting!" She sounded like she was going to burst with excitement.

"Can you transfer her through to me?" Mel heard Luce ask.

Mel prayed the girl would remember how to do it. All she had to remember was how to transfer to one number…

Persi pressed some buttons, which made noise but did nothing else. "I don't know!" she squeaked. Mel's heart sank.

"Then I'll just borrow your phone," Luce purred. His voice swelled in volume as he approached Persi's desk. "You don't mind if I lean over your desk, do you?" His tone didn't change after crackling noises told Mel the phone had changed hands. "Hello, Mel."

Mel shook her head, already worrying about the younger girl. Luce was laying it on a bit thick for poor Persi, especially with her so young and inexperienced. Bikies were fluffy bunnies compared to demons. "Hi. Lili's told me you need me for tonight's meeting. It starts at four in the boardroom, right?"

Luce laughed throatily. "That's right. Did she tell you that I'd require your services afterwards, finalising the minutes from the meeting and the like?"

Mel smiled in response, even though she knew he couldn't see her. "Of course. See you at four." She carefully placed the receiver back in the cradle.

Fifty-four

Four came around. Mel claimed the keyboard in the boardroom and time ticked away as she took the minutes for a thoroughly boring executive meeting. She kept her eyes on the screen and didn't look up, except to identify the presenter of a particular point.

"And for the very last time for a while, meeting adjourned!" she heard Luce say with some satisfaction, followed by a chorus of chairs pushing away from the table in unison. Heels and polished shoes tramped out the door to her cymbal-sigh of relief.

A pants-clad leg appeared on the table beside Mel. She sighed again and looked up as Luce beamed down at her.

"I had the girl order us dinner," he said with a wink. "I'll call the restaurant and tell them to deliver it."

Mel nodded wordlessly and returned her eyes to the screen. After one last check, she'd be done writing up the minutes, and free for the evening. She figured she might as well stay for dinner. At least until he'd reviewed the minutes so she could complete them.

She hit save as the leg returned. "Dinner's ready, dear," Luce said with a chuckle.

Mel glanced up. "I'm Mel, not Mephi or your wife. Can you check this over while I go find some cutlery?" She stood and walked out of the boardroom to the adjacent kitchen. She took her time selecting the cheapest plastic cutlery and giving it a wash first before returning to the boardroom.

Luce reclined in her still-warm seat, his eyes following her appreciatively as she entered the room. "It looks perfect to me."

"Good," Mel replied with a perfunctory

smile. She held up the white plastic knives and forks. "Where's the food?"

Luce rose. "In my office, of course." He led the way out.

Mel noticed he'd removed his jacket, so she had a clear view of his well-cut shirt and pants as she followed him. She wondered if she could get pants that showed off her behind so well. Shrugging, she dismissed the idea. Hell, she probably couldn't afford them, anyway.

"Your dinner," Luce said with a smile, gesturing at the meeting table in his office.

Room service, Mel thought. Of course.

The normally naked meeting table now wore a white tablecloth and dinner service for two, and Mel recognised the plates from the Christmas party at the Hilton. Her mouth watered at the sight of the chocolate raspberry mousse. She clutched at the plastic cutlery as she took in its stainless steel cousins on the white cloth.

"You won't be needing those." Luce nodded at her clenched fist of forks and friends. Mel released them onto the table, where they blended in with the cloth. He pulled back a chair for her and gestured for her to sit, before rounding the table to seat himself across from her.

Luce offered a bottle, tilting it over Mel's glass. "Wine?"

Mel's curiosity was piqued. "What kind?"

Luce shrugged. "Some white the hotel thinks goes well with the entrée."

So much for the suave, wine connoisseur of a CEO. Mel laughed outright as she tilted her head to read the label. She recognised it as one she liked but couldn't often afford, from the winery with the beautiful gardens down in Margaret River. "Yes."

The entrée was oysters. Mel didn't touch them.

Luce slurped through his before he noticed hers were untouched. "What's wrong with your oysters?" he asked through a mouthful.

Mel's stare was as cold as the bed of ice beneath their shells. "They're still alive."

"Not for long!" Luce grinned as he swallowed the last of his. He waited, but her expression didn't defrost. "Aren't you going to eat them?"

Mel lifted her wine glass and sipped, savouring the light wine. "No."

He reached for her plate. Slurp, slurp, slurp and Luce gulped his own wine with a grin, surveying the empty shells. "Do you know why I asked you to stay back tonight?" he asked.

Mel placed her glass carefully on the table. "Of course. It's your last day, as you're flying to take up some new position in the company that involves a lot of travel, and you wanted to check over the minutes before you left for good. I'm sorry I missed your farewell morning tea – I heard your speech was quite touching."

"Oh. Yes." Luce looked miffed, as if Mel had stolen his thunder. "Do you know why I'm leaving?"

Mel gave a small smile. "I had heard it was to do with your health…" She thought there might be some truth in that particular rumour, as the dark circles beneath his eyes betrayed him. She wondered what sort of malaise a demon could possibly suffer from.

Luce coughed. "Yes. The climate here is not what I'm used to. I need somewhere warmer, drier…"

"And with more smoke and sulphur?" Mel finished for him with a smile before she could stop herself.

"Where smoking is far less frowned upon than here, certainly," Luce replied uncertainly. It appeared Mel had stolen not just his thunder but his entire storm. "Shall we have the main course?"

"Sure. I'm starving," Mel said as she uncovered her plate. She thought longingly of the steak she had at home, but the one before her was seared and saucy, reclining on a bed of vegetables and crowned with a baby carrot. She tried not to laugh – he'd evidently asked the chef to make the meal as suggestive as possible, and so it was.

"More wine?" Luce said suddenly, grabbing a bottle of red and sloshing it into his own empty glass.

Mel drank the dregs of her white before tilting her glass toward him. "Please." The red ran smoothly into her glass, almost as dark as the steak. More Margaret River wine, but this time it was from Devil's Lair, Mel thought as she glanced at the label, tasting the unmistakeable shiraz.

Luce emptied his glass before Mel had set hers down, so he refilled it before tackling his meal. Mel smothered a smile and started slicing her steak into small pieces.

Mel kept her eyes down and Luce seemed to need to slurp his shiraz courage with increasing frequency. When she was sated, Mel carefully placed her cutlery side by side on the plate. She carefully wiped her parted lips with her cloth napkin before delicately taking another sip of wine.

"I want you to come with me. I need you," Luce blurted out. His knuckles were white as he clutched the empty wine bottle.

Mel touched her wineglass to her lips once more, holding the rich red in her mouth for a few moments before swallowing. "I'm needed here."

Luce swallowed and tried again with some difficulty. Mel wondered if he'd had too much wine. "I need a personal assistant in my new job and I want you. I'll be travelling a lot, incorporating new acquisitions into the HELL Corporation. I'll need an absolute angel who can do anything to be my assistant – an angel like you."

Mel smiled. "Like me? Would another angel do?" Her heart went out to the demon, but she knew this was the perfect opportunity to replace herself in his affections or whatever his feelings for her were.

Luce looked uncertain. "What do you mean?"

Mel tried to keep the wickedness from her smile. "Well, only half-angel, really. Your new PA, Persephone, is perfect for what you need. She's far more helpful than I could ever be. She'll keep everything in order to the last detail – she'll be able to tell if you're missing a pomegranate seed from your breakfast."

"You mean the girl with the glasses? A half-angel, really? What's the other half?" Luce looked stunned. Perhaps it was the wine.

Mel permitted herself to laugh. "My cousin – her mother – insisted that he was some sort of Greek god, but he was about as much use as a marble statue. I didn't enquire further." Her smile turned prim. "You might want to ask Persephone about her halo."

"But you said your cousin isn't a full angel. How can she have a real halo on her head?" Luce asked, laughing.

"Ah, no, not on her head," Mel replied, biting her lip so she didn't say any more. He evidently hadn't persuaded Persi onto his desk yet, or he'd know exactly what she was referring to. "She's even a fan of unusual art, like the pictures on your wall. You'll like Persephone." And she might like him, if his tongue was smoother than it was tonight. Mel reached for her dish of mousse and dipped her spoon. Heavenly, as before. She resolved to learn to make this, for she could hardly afford dessert from the Hilton every day.

"Are you sure you want to refuse my offer?" Luce watched Mel.

She felt sorry for him, but she'd promised Raphael and Persephone that she'd leave him to them. Her sympathy for the demon was clouding her judgement. Time to make good on her word.

Mel dropped her spoon in her dish. "Yes. My place is here." She wiped her lips with the soft cloth once more before dropping that, too. Mel stood and Luce mirrored her movement. He looked so forlorn; she pitied the demon more than she thought possible. Perhaps it was best that Persi would be his downfall and not her. She didn't have the heart to rip out his.

Mel rounded the table to his side. On impulse, she kissed his ruddy cheek. "Farewell, Luce. Thank you for the lovely dinner and the orchids you sent me secretly for Valentine's Day. I wish you the best, both in your new job and your health. If your travels bring you back to my city, I'd love to catch up again for dinner and drinks. Persi will know how to get into contact with me." She stepped away from him. "Now, I must go home to get some sleep."

"I have a couch here. We could share!" Luce shouted after her, more than an edge of desperation in his tone.

No, Persi would not share. Even a prince of darkness would be putty in her pretty hands in this state. And her halo…oh Hell!

"Goodnight, Luce."

Mel fought her laughter as she left the building, laughing so loud and hard on the train that the other passengers gave her a wide berth, which was just as well. If she stopped laughing, she'd cry. The lost, lonely look on his face as she left had smote her heart. She hadn't even been able to say her final goodbye.

Fifty-five

She hated to admit it, but the office was dull without Luce. The work was the same, but it seemed to lack a vibrancy that she now thought had stemmed from his presence. It wasn't that she missed him – all the demons seemed to be more somnolent. Of course, that could be partly because there'd been some incident with the delivery truck so that there weren't any coffee beans left – and there wouldn't be any more until the following Tuesday.

Lili seemed to ask less of her, while she

spent longer and longer at lunch or generally away from the office. More than once, there were new shopping bags on Lili's filing cabinet in the afternoons. Perhaps there was some truth in the rumour that Lili was Luce's mistress, for she definitely seemed to be pining away for something.

Mel shut down her PC and headed home. Today Persi was due to call in her first weekly report and Mel was curious about the girl's progress.

The call lasted fifteen minutes. Persi used the word "fine" at least thirty times by Mel's tally and asked more questions than she answered. She wanted to know how Luce liked his coffee, what his favourite foods were, and whether he preferred her to initiate sex or would she have to wait for orders. Mel almost choked on her tea at this last one, before she managed to suggest that Persi try taking the initiative. Evidently Luce hadn't liked the desk in his hotel room, or Mel was sure Persi would have spread herself across it at even the slightest suggestion that he wanted sex. Persi was certainly no angel in that respect.

The only question she did answer, fortunately, was the most important. "What sort of deal did he sign at the meeting yesterday?"

"Some sort of agreement to provide government services in the United States," Persi said slowly. "Health services, I think. I didn't think the US government provided health services…but he has a meeting tomorrow with some fancy real estate agent about office space. Not just here, but all over the world. Donald Dump or something, I think he said his name was…" She giggled.

Glancing at the itinerary Persi had given her, Mel decided to pay the two a visit and see precisely how fine their business was in…New York, she read, and they were staying at what appeared to be called the Trump hotel – not a dump at all. Ah, she'd soon find out.

Mel stretched out to sleep, feeling her spirit shake free of her tired body. As a pure angel, with no human limitations aside from the universe's laws of physics, she could swim through the atmosphere as sentient light. She couldn't leave her body for long, as the constructed form would start to disintegrate if untended, but an hour or two would be more than enough time to travel to New York and back – far faster than flying in any aircraft. She'd check on the couple and return home, with no one the wiser. Better yet, she'd be invisible to human eyes in her angel form.

She revelled in the refreshing sensation of fast flight and it felt like mere seconds before the trees of a very different Central Park appeared below her, in chilly morning sunlight. The snow surprised her, until she realised the reversed seasons and higher latitude placed the park in very early spring. She'd been working for the HELL Corporation so long, she'd missed winter in Korea, too.

She reached out, for she knew Persi's soul well. The agitated girl was in a hotel room overlooking the park and Mel could hear Luce's voice, complaining that she'd picked the wrong hotel. He never accepted favours from Trump, though he offered his hotel every time. Something about the rich Carlton…no, the Ritz-Carlton.

"But they had no suites left with park views,

sir, and you said you needed both…" Persi whined. "Let me help you with that, sir."

Mel would have laughed at the repeated "sirs" but she was trying to stay as subdued as possible. Luce might be able to sense another spirit in the room — and she didn't want to be seen.

She couldn't see Persi at first — just Luce, sitting at a desk, frowning at his laptop, a cup of coffee on the glass surface beside him. The dark circles beneath his eyes seemed to have worsened in the week he'd been away — jet lag, she presumed.

Persi was…under the desk, plugging in the laptop power cable. "I see something else I can do for you, sir," she said. Mel heard unzipping, then slurping, as she realised precisely what Persi was doing for Luce. Luce shifted uncomfortably in his seat, nudging her away with his foot and Mel heard Persi's voice say thickly, "Oh, please, sir…"

Mel felt a desire to gag — quite a feat without a throat or digestive tract. Where in Hell had Persi learned to be so sickeningly submissive?

"Fine. Make it quick," Luce grunted, closing

the document he was working on. Instead, he opened a presentation and Mel's attention was drawn to the screen. He'd pulled up the picture of her in her wet swimsuit in Sri Lanka and his eyes were fixed on the picture with an intensity that made Mel blush – or it would have, had she brought a body.

To Mel's relief, Persi did indeed make it quick, crawling out from under the table less than five minutes later, wiping her mouth. "If you like, sir, I'd be happy to provide a more complete service any time you please. Whenever and wherever." She winked, but Luce wasn't looking at her. He'd quickly opened up his email and was scrolling through one message so slowly that Mel wondered if he was trying to memorise it. She looked closer – it was the email she'd sent him with her Sri Lanka photos.

"Get out," Luce said shortly. "We leave for our first meeting in an hour and I need to work without interruptions until then. Close the door behind you. I'll grab you when it's time."

Persi pouted and glided to the door to her

adjoining room. "If you're sure…" she purred, lifting her skirt a little to give Luce a lovely glimpse of her tattooed skin.

Luce didn't even look.

The door closed quietly as Persi slumped onto the bucket chair in her room. After a minute, she headed to the bathroom to brush her teeth – twice, Mel guessed, as it took so long and required a significant amount of spitting. Mel slipped back into Luce's room, wondering what work was so secret that it couldn't proceed in front of Persi.

Luce's fingers stroked the sunset shot on the LCD screen as he murmured, "My God, what I'd do for a single ray of your sunshine, Mel."

Stunned, Mel tried to shrink back into Persi's room. He was more perceptive than she'd realised – and she'd tried to be so careful…

He buried his head in his hands. "It should be you here instead of that…that…little lamprey. I'd take five minutes in the same room as you over a whole night naked with her. Hell, I'd give Trump back his millions and tear up the contracts if it meant you could be

here. I'd give anything. Anything. Ah Hell..."
He crossed to the bar fridge and extracted a
small bottle of amber liquid. He wrenched it
open and poured the contents into his coffee,
then drank it down in three gulps that sounded
surprisingly like sobs. "Melody..."

Luce's soul writhed like a nest of snakes
having a violent orgy. In her spirit form, Mel
could see the turmoil more clearly than ever
before. He gritted his teeth against the pain.
"I'll take this corporation global and then I'll
come back for you, Mel. You won't have to be
a temp, doing Lili's dirty work in a boring little
city far from everywhere. You can have any
job you want in any city you please. I'll give
you the world...even if you don't want me."

Wishing she could help or even say
something to comfort him and knowing she
couldn't, Mel swept out, winging her way
home to where she knew Luce wanted to be.
She resolved not to look in on him again – it
broke her heart to see the demon so lonely.
And the way he'd said her name...Much more
of this and she couldn't help stepping in – she
couldn't bear to see such suffering.

Of course, it could all be a front to win her sympathy and enslave her soul, Mel mused as she passed the Equator. If he'd suspected she was in his hotel room, he could have lied through his perfect teeth. Luce had a reputation for being the most seductive demon there was and he was certainly arrogant enough to make the attempt. She kept thinking of the storm in his soul, though, for that had been real. Luce was at war with himself – that she knew for certain.

She'd promised she'd stay out of it until Persi needed her help. And the girl couldn't help but fail, with Luce like this.

In the meantime, Persi was her responsibility – and she would watch over the girl as carefully as she could, while avoiding the depressed demon next door.

Mel settled back into her body, rousing from slumber so she could shift it from the bed to the phone.

Flexing her fingers, she dialled Raphael's number and heard his sleepy voice. "Mm? Mel? What is it?"

"Persi called. This isn't just a fact-finding

mission like you thought – the meetings are contract negotiations. Luce is taking the HELL Corporation global. He's sourced offices in several countries and he already has a signed contract with the US government – for their health services, the largest portfolio in their budget."

"Oh Hell."

"We need to gain control of HELL Corporation and remove Lucifer. Do you want to tell Persi? She'll have to get him to sign the documents somehow."

Mel could almost hear Raphael thinking, before he finally said, "You tell Persi what she needs to do. I'll have some of our legal boys draft the contracts. Tell her to sell herself into slavery if she has to – but she needs to get him to sign those documents, whatever the cost."

"I draw the line at her soul, Raphael. Her body is hers to do what she wants with, but I won't support her selling her soul."

"Hers or yours, Mel – I'd hand hers over any day. It's a fair price to pay to thwart Lucifer in his bid for this much power."

Mel sighed. She'd have preferred to proceed

differently – with Luce's soul as the bargaining chip – but it was out of her hands now. At least, it was for the moment. "When she calls next, I'll tell her. You have a week to produce watertight contracts. Ones even American lawyers can't find loopholes in."

Fifty-Six

"Are you a first aid officer?" a harried-looking man asked Mel.

She put down her phone reluctantly, her mind still on the book about a writer's romance. "Yes. What's happened?" She rose from her seat.

The man led the way through the cubicle maze. "We've had another incident in the store room. One bloke's unconscious and bleeding on the floor, while one of the girls from HR has injured her wrist, apparently with one of her heels. She says that the injury was sustained in self-defence…"

Mel hurried after him, her own heels padding on the carpeted floor. Something seemed very strange today.

The HR manager walked past, clutching a file to her chest and shaking her head. "This is bad, very bad. It's the third one today – the tenth this week – and it's only Tuesday…" she muttered to no one in particular.

She reached the doorway of the store room and stopped, stunned.

A man was indeed unconscious on the carpet; his head and shoulders had landed on the bottom of one of the shelving units. Through his forearm was a red stiletto heel, the gel cushion insert hanging out like the man's tongue. Black blood seeped from his arm onto the pile of telephone message pads beneath him.

An hysterical Ana clutched a ream of paper to her chest, the fingers of one hand wrapped around the wrist of her other hand. "He deserved it! Thieving policy officer…"

Mel noticed blood and some of the man's equally dark hair sticking to the wrapper around the ream of paper.

She summoned a soothing smile and reached past Ana for one of the first aid kits. Without taking her eyes off the hysterical woman or the limp man, Mel said over her shoulder, "Could you call me an ambulance, please?" She looked at Ana, who had kicked off her other red heel, looking ready to use it. "Make that two ambulances, for two casualties?"

"Sure," the other man replied as he hurried away.

"May I?" Mel asked, extending her hand to Ana.

"You can't have it! We're completely out!" Ana shouted.

Mel smiled her most angelic smile. "Not the paper. I'd like to examine your wrist."

Mel prodded for a moment until the woman yanked her hand back with an cry of pain. "It looks like a bad sprain. Best get you to hospital. Did you want to go wait in Reception?"

Ana gave a curt nod. "Right after I get this paper in the printer." She marched off to HR, still hugging her bloody ream of paper.

Mel turned her attention to the man on the floor. She didn't know him, but she didn't expect to – there were plenty of HELL Corporation policy officers she hadn't met. She hoped he'd recover enough from his head injury to be able to tell her his name. Sighing, she lightly patted his face and hands. "Wake up, please, and tell me if you can hear me. Are you okay?"

The man groaned and moved, but he didn't say anything she understood, so Mel repeated the exercise.

"Ffff…ucking bitch," the man mumbled after a while.

Mel pressed her lips together. "Can you tell me your name?"

"Mo," he mumbled.

"Mo? Your name is Mo?"

"Yyy…sss," Mo replied with difficulty.

"Right, well, I'm Mel and I've called you an ambulance, which will take you to hospital so you can get checked out."

"Good. Call….p...lice…too," he mumbled.

"We're sorting that out right now," Mel said

carefully.

Luckily, the ambulance officers didn't take long to arrive and they took Mo away, relieving Mel of her responsibilities. She headed back to her desk, detouring to wash Mo's blood off her hands first.

Lili appeared, looking flustered. "Oh, Mel! Could you sort and staple these documents in time for my meeting in five minutes?" She dumped the ream of printed paper on Mel's desk and wandered off without waiting for Mel's answer.

With a sigh, Mel pulled out her stapler and started dealing with the sheets.

She made it to a third of the way through before her stapler protested and died. Patiently, Mel tapped it on the desk and checked the staples. She added some more, just in case. The stapler didn't do anything.

She peered into it and thought perhaps a staple had gotten jammed. She tried to pry it out with a pair of scissors, but they were too big. She needed something smaller, like…

Mel picked up a pen and inserted the point into her stapler, trying to get the wayward staple out. The pen point snapped, shattering the plastic with it. Mel dropped the pen into the bin by the desk. She searched her desk for a letter opener or something else she could use, but came up with nothing.

She headed over to Merih's desk. "How do I order a new stapler and a pen to replace the ones I just broke?" she asked.

He shrugged. "You can't. You have to fix them or do without."

She stared at him. "What? I can't have a new pen?"

He pulled up the internal network screen and tapped his monitor. "That's why."

"...the Minister has issued a media statement announcing immediate saving measures across government. These measures include: a temporary freeze on all expenditure on the procurement of non-essential goods and services (consumables such as stationery, use of consultants, non-essential travel)," she read. Mel looked at Merih. "But stationery is essential! This is an office!"

Merih shrugged. "Apparently not, according to the Minister. Haven't you noticed the fights breaking out in the store room where the stationery used to be kept?"

Oh.

Two hours later, Mel had taken her stapler apart, sustaining several bleeding cuts in the process, and reassembled it so it worked once more. Leaving bloody fingerprints on the documents, she finished dealing with the papers and delivered them to Lili's meeting. Then she went in search of a first aid kit to clean and cover her cuts.

By that time, the work day was over. She slipped her phone into her bag and lifted it onto her shoulder.

She'd wasted a whole work day over ten dollars' worth of stationery – a stapler and a ream of paper. That was…almost three hundred dollars of wasted time and money. How was that saving?

Hell will freeze over before she found out, Mel decided. Her laughter bubbled up as she realised the reality. No, Hell had already frozen over. On the Minister's orders.

Fifty-Seven

"No, there's no more paper," Lili said before Mel could even ask why her documents hadn't printed. "We used our last ream yesterday and I swear I saw one of the Environment boys stealing from our printer this morning. No one wastes as much paper as the Environment Division…" She hungrily eyed the pen in Mel's hand. "You're lucky you still have a pen. Everyone else's went missing overnight."

"Actually, I have two. If you need one…" Mel offered her pen and Lili snatched it from her. Mel sighed. "Is the Minister's freeze still in effect? I don't see how it affects us. It's not like the government's paying for our stationery – I thought the HELL Corporation costs were factored into your initial bid to provide services..."

Lili shrugged. "It's the look of the thing. All government departments are making funding cuts to allow for renovations to the premier's new palace to include a brothel in the basement. They say it'll save millions, but not before it's open for business. We can't look like we're spending lots of money when all the other government services are skimping..."

Mel smothered a laugh. "I still think there are better ways to save money than not allowing us to have stationery. I can't get anything done."

"Go get a coffee," Lili suggested. "Maybe by the time you're back, Merih and Gerry will have scrounged enough paper to print."

Mel nodded, but bypassed the kitchen for the stairs up to the executive suite. Luce wouldn't have agreed to such stupid austerity measures and she'd be damned before she'd sit around and do nothing, wasting their money by doing no work.

Mel was surprised to see Mephi back, not to mention smiling blissfully and humming. Had it really been a month since she'd left? Luce had been gone for just as long. The office was definitely a different place without him. Mel found she actually missed the man. His conversation, more than anything, as well as the occasional coffee he'd made for her. Coffee and conversation. Mel tried not to laugh. She was certain Luce would have preferred that she miss parts of his personality and anatomy that started with C, though Persi was probably doing her best to ensure he forgot all about Mel. And so she should.

"Mel! Oh, you won't believe how wonderful it was! Bob and I…we…were arrested by the Japanese police." Mephi blushed, looking absurdly proud.

Mel wasn't sure whether to laugh, smile or look concerned. "I'm happy to hear you enjoyed your holiday. I hope it was all a misunderstanding," she said carefully.

Mephi giggled, sounding eerily like Persi instead of her usual efficient self. "Public nudity, disturbing the peace, property damage, inciting public violence, rioting, misuse of public property…oh, it was incredible. Bob and I spent half the night naked on the futons, but we got too hot and decided to try a romp in the snow. My knees went numb, so I insisted we visit the hot springs, but the indoor ones wouldn't let us in together, because they keep men and women separate – can you imagine? So we found some up the hill that were outdoors and not segregated…"

Mel coughed. "Up the hill…you mean the cooking hot springs? The ones that are too hot for humans, with all the warning signs?"

"Humans, maybe, but they were just a warm bath to us demons, dear. And we steamed them up a fair bit more before we were done. So we had another roll in the snow…and fell through someone's basement window. We climbed out, had another wash in the hot springs – just to disinfect, of course, the cuts from the broken glass, but one thing led to another and…by that time some of the townspeople were up and they were very rude, so Bob broke off a length of the chain fence and used it to protect me..." Mephi's eyes misted over at the memory.

"Wow. Sounds like an exciting holiday," Mel managed to say. She didn't think she'd ever understand demons.

"It was." Mephi sighed. "What can I do for you, dear? Just name it. Bob and I will be in your debt for eternity."

Mel took a deep breath. "I'd like to see whoever's doing Luce's job. I want to discuss the austerity measures."

"Let me just check..." Mephi frowned at her monitor. "He's free now and for the next half hour. Go right in."

He sat at Luce's desk. The office looked no different, but the man who occupied it was a shadow compared to the charismatic Lord of Hell. "What is it?" he asked, rubbing his face with both hands as he looked up. "And who are you?"

"I'm Mel," she began. "I want to hear it from you – why the entire corporation is under these austerity measures. I'd like to assist, but I can't unless I know why."

He shuffled through the papers piled up

over his desk. Luce had never had that much paper in his entire office, let alone his desk. "There was a memo from the Minister. I had Mephi send it around…"

Mel wet her lips. "Oh yes, I saw that. It doesn't explain why. The HELL Corporation's profits are rising steadily and it's picking up more government services every week. The only reason I can think of is the need for capital elsewhere – if Luce is thinking of expanding his corporation on a global scale. If this is the case, then reducing its productivity here by not ordering paper is pointless."

Cold, dark eyes regarded her, but he didn't say a word.

"You've got an office full of staff, fighting over stationery and doing nothing else. Half of them are spending their entire work day stealing paper from the other half, who are out on coffee and smoke breaks because they can't do anything else. Zero productivity will only make the company look bad when Luce wants it to appear at its best, in the media and otherwise. All it'll take is one person to talk to the media and the press will be all over it – and office humour like this will go viral, reaching the furthest corners of the globe wherever Luce is. Luce wouldn't have authorised this and he'd stop it if he knew."

The man folded his arms. "Are you threatening to talk to the press or Lucifer? He left me in charge and said that anyone who doesn't follow orders will go right back to the Pit for insubordination or inciting trouble. That's a Level Eight offence – and you'll be on the receiving end for as long as I see fit." His demonic grin was the picture of fierce anticipation.

"I'm agency staff," Mel replied coolly. "If you want me to work outside of the CBD, you'll have to renegotiate my contract with the agency and I have to agree to it. Keep your threats for the staff you can control. Admittedly, if you don't have any stationery in the office, there's really no point in me or any of the agency staff being here, as our productivity is worse than that of your regular, demonic staff. You see, we fill out paper timesheets that have to be signed by hand. At the end of this week, if there's no paper to print our timesheets, we won't be working because, unlike demons, we don't do anything based on empty threats and no reward."

"Fine. You're fired, then," he said, waving his hand as if ridding himself of a bad smell.

Mel kept her face expressionless, despite her initial desire to smile. If she wasn't required to spend all day in the office at the demons' beck and call, she could keep better track of Luce and Persi – and be available to fly out the moment Persi called for help.

After a moment, she nodded. "I suggest you terminate the contracts of all agency staff at the end of this week and use the money for stationery. Luce will thank you for it – instead of sending you to whatever level of Hell is reserved for idiots who waste resources." She turned on her heel and left.

She heard the man scramble to his feet and follow her. "Mephi!" he called. "Send a note to…whoever. Tell them to fire all the agency staff."

"But, Bob…that's Mel. She's the angel who suggested our holiday destination. You can't…" Mephi protested.

Mel stopped. "It's all right," she said. "We're all temporary staff and we're only here for as long as we're needed. The agency will have another assignment before I reach home tonight, I'm sure of it."

Mephi drew herself up, shedding all semblance of humanity. Mel watched in fascination as the immaculate skirt split to reveal a well-muscled red leg that matched the demon's furious face. A ruddy finger stabbed the air to emphasise each word. "Beelzebub! How DARE you. I won't let you send Mel out of here in disgrace after what she did for us…for our marriage! If you EVER want me to touch you again, you will see to it that she has a job for life or a proper send off – WHATEVER she asks for. And if she asks for your gift-wrapped genitals as a going-away gift…I will tie the blood-spattered bow myself!"

The man in the suit seemed to shrink. "Yes, dear."

Mel smiled politely. "A morning tea would be plenty. As for a fitting farewell gift…a pen is fine. Something small to remember you all by."

Mephi's skin faded to normal. "I'll see to it that catering is ordered for ten on Friday. We'll miss you, Mel."

Mel couldn't say the same, so she said what she could: "Thank you."

Fifty-eight

Merih cleared his throat noisily. "We all want to thank you for everything you've done. The quality of the coffee. The wording of our laws and policies. The paper-purchasing freeze. The protesters. The training sessions. The CEO's end-of-year presentation. Saving us all from aliens. Saving the CEO from a swan. Mephi and Bob's second honeymoon. And who can forget the chocolates on Valentine's Day? Everything you've touched here is better because you've been with us. We want to thank you in the best way we know how. Now, every man among us wants to give you a good six inches…"

"And the ladies," Ana said under her breath, lifting her six inch stiletto heel.

"Or more!" shouted Nybbas, turning red.

"Or more," agreed Merih, "but we figured we'd give you something just as long and hard that lasts longer than five minutes. Something to remember us by."

He handed her a small, gift-wrapped box, dwarfed by the huge card accompanying it. Mel smiled, thanked him, and opened the card first. It was full of tiny writing – from what looked like all the staff she'd ever met, or given chocolate to on Valentine's Day. Tears sprang to her eyes. "Thank you," she said again.

"Open it!" Gerry hollered. "Ana said what you needed most was a vibrator because you'd never see any action any other way. We all want to see what sort of sex toy fits in a box that small!"

Mel laughed and blushed. "If you insist." She unwrapped the paper with care and pulled out the box. "Ohhh…that's so kind of you. What a lovely surprise. I want to use it right away…"

"Is it a gift voucher for the sex shop on Murray Street?" Ana asked loudly.

"No. Much better than that. It's a beautiful pen," Mel said, holding up the gold writing implement so the light caught it.

"We had your name engraved on it, too," Merih murmured, pointing at the three letters that spelled out her name, to her relief.

Her tears escaped. "Thank you so much."

"SPEECH!" Nybbas bellowed.

"I…I can't," Mel whispered as every demonic eye settled on her. Forcing herself not to run and hide, she tried to clear her throat to find her voice. If she closed her eyes, perhaps she could.

"Thank you. Thank you so much. I hope…I only hope I helped."

There was silence as the demons waited for more words – perhaps they wanted something like Luce's long speeches, but Mel had no more.

Clapping started behind her and someone whistled. The room erupted in applause and Mel dared to open her eyes. It was over. Her time in HELL was over.

It hadn't been so bad after all. Who'd have thought?

Fifty-nine

"Morning, Mel. I need your help. How do I…"

"I swallowed a whole German sausage in front of him and he barely blinked! Every other man in the place offered me a job or a bed, but Luce locked me out of his room! What else do I have to do to…"

"What do I do if…"

"He said I have to wear a scarf over my head for the meeting. He said I can't go unless I cover up. How am I supposed to seduce him if the only skin I can show is my face without any makeup? Help me, Mel, I don't know how to…"

"We had to drink this foul-tasting brown spirit that burned all the way down. I coughed so hard I lost my voice. What should I do tonight so I don't…"

"We're meeting with the Treasury Minister in London tomorrow. I have all the documents prepared, just like you said. Do you really think I should open the meeting with…"

Mel kept her voice calm and kept talking until she knew Persi had understood. "What you need to do is…"

Every day. Sometimes two or three times a day. Constant phone calls, text messages and emails. Persi would panic and Mel was her panacea. Mel longed for the day that she was only a placebo, so she could wean the girl off her blind obedience. She needed so many instructions just to get through the day…

Yet the girl was improving – and she was trying to look after Luce, too. Mel couldn't bring herself to turn a completely blind eye to Luce, even if she only saw him through Persi's panicked perception. Persi made sure he was always on time and immaculately dressed, that he ate and drank, and that his coffee was perfect. She vetted the restaurant menus and presented them to Mel until she learned what Luce liked to eat.

Mel didn't how she'd have managed to do this on top of her daily drudgery at the office, and was doubly glad she didn't work for the HELL Corporation anymore.

Day by day, she wondered when she'd receive Persi's resignation — when would the girl admit defeat? So many of her questions were about how to attract Luce — despite her repeated offers, Luce wouldn't sleep with the girl and he'd threatened to find a new PA if she crawled under the desk or into his bed again.

Luce without lust — Mel couldn't help laughing at the very thought of it, for it was so hard to believe. The demon she knew would have happily taken any willing girl on his desk here in Perth — what had left him so impotent now?

With every phone call, her understanding deepened and Mel wished again that she'd disregarded Raphael's advice and accepted Luce's offer. She'd be holding his soul in her hands by now, instead of having to talk Persi through even the simplest of negotiations. Or offering the girl advice on seducing a man she'd never slept with, and didn't intend to.

The front windows rattled ominously thanks to yet another strong gust of wind. Mel paid little attention to it – her windows had withstood sixty years of such storms and the glass was only a little loose in the frames. She was more worried that she'd lose power before the kettle boiled for her cup of tea. She'd developed quite a taste for her floral tisanes and she wanted her drink in hand when Persi called again.

The rain pelting on the tin roof drowned out all other sound for a few minutes – she only knew the kettle was ready because the light had switched off. Dropping one of the tiny pyramid teabags into her cup, she tipped the kettle to pour her tea. The smell of jasmine steam made her smile as she closed her eyes, simply enjoying the scent. Even angels were allowed guilty pleasures such as this. She lifted the cup and took a small sip.

The downpour desisted and Mel heard the rattling again – this time, both her windows and the front door. That was unusual – for a wind gust to swirl through her carport and reach the door, it would have to move around corners.

"Mel!" she heard a voice sob. "You have to let me in. I don't know who else to turn to. Please help me!"

The door shuddered in its frame as Mel realised it wasn't just the wind knocking at her door in the storm.

"Please, Mel!"

She sighed and set down her tea. No one should be out in such a storm – especially not someone who knew her name and address.

She turned both locks and swung the front

door open.

"Oh, thank God. Please let me in, Mel. I'll do anything."

She couldn't see his face in the carport shadows, but pity drove her not to care. She unlatched the screen door and swung it out into the darkness. "Come in. You must be soaked."

He stumbled on the steps and she held out her hand to help him. His wet fingers closed gratefully over hers as he stepped over the threshold.

Mel stood back to stare. It had been weeks since she'd last seen Luce and those weeks had not been kind to him. His suit sagged from his shoulders under the weight of water it held, the smell of wet wool overpowering the delicate scent of jasmine tea. His hair, plastered to his head, dripped down his face, highlighting the dark circles beneath his eyes. He folded his arms across his body, trying to stop the shivering. "Thank you," he said.

"What happened?" she asked carefully. She suspected she knew, but that didn't explain how he was here, in her house.

"She…that devil woman…took everything. Slowly at first and then…I had no control any more. Do you know she has a halo on her…on her…and she wanted me to…" His eyes widened in horror, yet the horrors could only be in his head.

Mel noticed the puddle forming on her carpet at his feet. She touched a cautious hand to his back. "You should get out of those drenched clothes and into something warm and dry. How about you take a shower while I see if I have anything that might fit you." She guided him to the sunny yellow bathroom and closed the door.

Pressing her lips together, she headed for the guest room, where she kept the clothes Raphael had left at her house – he could certainly spare them. Particularly if it was his fault there was a man in her house who needed them. With the weight Luce appeared to have lost, he'd have no trouble fitting into Raphael's clothes.

She took a shirt, pants and a sweater to the bathroom, rapping on the timber door with her knuckles. "I have some clothes for you," she called. She couldn't hear the water running, so she cracked the door open a little and passed the pile of folded garments through the gap.

Luce's hands covered Mel's briefly before he took her offering. "Thank you."

Once her hands were empty, she quickly pulled the door closed. "Let me know if you need anything else. Use as much hot water as you like. The towels are clean – I brought them in from the line just before the storm hit." She waited for the hiss of the shower starting before she strode to her bedroom with grim purpose.

Picking up her phone from the charger, she noticed a missed call from the one person she needed to speak to, timed to match the beginning of the downpour.

The line rang twice before it was answered. "Hell—"

Mel cut her off. "How goes your assignment?"

Persi giggled. "Mission accomplished. I now have control of all his interests in the HELL Corporation."

"At what cost?" Mel ground her teeth.

"Almost nothing. It felt too easy, Mel. I barely had to do anything – I didn't even have to sleep with him in the end. It was like he just gave up."

"What was his price?" Mel asked urgently.

"Just your phone number and home address. Nothing!" Persi insisted. "He's powerless now, Mel. It's not like you have to answer, talk to him or even let him in. He doesn't matter any more."

Mel thought of how the demons in the office had responded to Luce – like marionettes to a puppeteer. He could sign over everything in the world to Persi, but he was still the unchallenged master of Hell and all it contained. It was both his strength and his curse. "You're wrong. He does matter." Mel heard the water in the shower stop flowing. "Report to Raphael. Tell him your assignment is complete – earlier than expected, too. Convey my congratulations to you both on a job well done. I'll finish up here." She terminated the call, taking a deep breath to strengthen herself. She had a damp demon to deal with.

Sixty-one

Mel settled onto the sofa, sipping her still-warm tea. She set a second, steaming cup on the coffee table for Luce.

The floorboards outside the bathroom door creaked under his weight, drawing her eyes from the cup to her guest. Raphael's shirt was too big and the pants would have fallen off him if he didn't have a belt. He looked slightly less lost now.

"You kept them," he said in wonder.

"I did?" Mel asked, unsure.

He nodded slowly. "The flowers. The

orchids I…secretly bought you for Valentine's Day, but you knew, all the same. I thought you didn't like them. Yet…you took them home and cared for them. They look as perfect as they were in February. Surely those can't be the same flowers!"

Mel smiled. "They are. They seem to like my bathroom. Perhaps it's the humidity." She took another sip of her tea so she could avoid his eyes. The intensity of his gaze was more than a little disconcerting.

"It's you. You breathe the tiniest whisper of your vitality into everything around you and it's as if the whole world comes to life. Even I feel better and I'm…I'm…"

Mel waited for Luce to finish his sentence, but he didn't seem able to. "Please, sit down. Have some tea."

Luce nodded and accepted, inhaling deeply as he sank into an armchair. He slurped the hot liquid. "This is good," he said in surprise.

Mel nodded, taking a deep draught of her own. After swallowing, she said, "I'd like you to tell me again what happened. Take as much time as you need and, please, don't hold back on details. You mentioned a devil woman with a halo?"

Luce nodded, lowering his cup from his lips. "Your…cousin. The half-angel. Persephone. Oh God, she was my PA. The perfect assistant, just like you said she'd be. She kept my schedule so well I only had to ask her to know exactly where I should be. She knew it all. New York, Berlin, Singapore, Johannesburg, Dubai…she had my coffee in hand before I knew I needed it. Took the minutes, prepared all the documents…read them so she could brief me on the plane, or assist me in the meetings. Then London…she effortlessly took control of the negotiation. And when we got back to the hotel, we had adjoining hotel rooms and she left the door open. When I got out of the shower, she was naked on my bed. She spread her legs and…she has a…a…" Luce swallowed and looked horrified.

"Halo tattoo?" she suggested, not needing a graphic description.

"Y…yeah," he managed to say. "I took one look at her and I couldn't. You marked me, so

I felt nothing for her. Nothing!"

This was news to her. Mel tilted her head. "I marked you? When, and how?"

The disconcerted demon blushed. "When you kissed me goodbye. An angel's kiss is redemption for us. You gave it willingly, without…and you wished me well! It took me a fortnight to figure it out – what you'd done to me with that one touch. While I was distracted, she just took more and more until, one day, she asked me to sign over everything to her. The company and everything I owned. So I did – if she'd tell me how to find you again."

A redeemed demon? Could there be such a thing? Mel could think of only one thing that could cause such a transformation and it wasn't her farewell kiss. It might help explain his obvious ill-health, too. Not to mention why he'd been stroking pictures of her on his laptop in New York. Mel regarded him over the rim of her cup as she drank the remainder of her tea. Did the man know the source of the sickness in his soul? She'd never seen a soul at war with itself before.

She kept her voice light as she said, "It was hardly a kiss. A peck on the cheek, perhaps. An angel's kiss usually annihilates your kind, or sends you back into the Pit. You were Persi's charge, not mine, and you seemed so happy to have her. Yet you left her and came here in the middle of a storm. Why?" Even as she tilted her head, she kept her eyes on him.

Luce flashed a rueful smile. "I left so quickly, I barely noticed the storm start. I didn't want to turn back and return to her. I just wanted to find you." He held out his hand. "Here, let me get you another cup of tea."

Mel surrendered her empty mug and watched him carry both his and hers to the kitchen. She'd left the box of tea on the counter, so he didn't have to hunt for it. Ten minutes later, he returned, carrying two steaming cups.

She inclined her head in thanks as she accepted her drink, setting it on the table to cool. "Give me your hand. I want to see this for myself."

Luce swallowed, almost choking on his tea. "You want to see my soul? Why?"

"I want to understand better. I have seen it all before, Luce," Mel replied, trying not to laugh. "Yes, even yours. Remember? In front of the swans on the foreshore, before you told dirty jokes to try and make me blush."

"You didn't blush. The other angel did. You laughed." Luce looked at her, as if conducting some form of assessment. He came to a decision and held out both shaking hands, palms up. Mel took them. She drew a deep breath and looked into his eyes for a long time. "Your eyes are still just as beautiful," he murmured, but Mel shushed him.

The war was over – but which side had won? Mel wondered. Oh, my…

She released his hands first; shaking her head when she was done reading his soul. "I don't understand. How can the shadow on your soul be simply…gone? Changed, somehow. It looks almost as clean as an angel's. How can you be the demon who tried to seduce me in the boardroom, your office, the work Christmas party…how can you change this much?"

He grinned. "I told you, you marked me.

And you're partly right. I'm not redeemed yet – not completely, anyway. I'm toying with the idea of pinning you to the couch, ripping your clothes off and having my wicked way with you. I still might."

Decisively un-demon-like, Mel mused. A normal demon, like the Luce she knew, would have seduced her out of her clothes and waited for her to ask (or beg) for him. Demons didn't do rape – their aim was to damn the soul they seduced. Luce sounded more like a lusty human than a demon – and he didn't seem to realise it. Her suspicions swirled, coalescing into very curious thought-clouds.

Mel took up her cup again. "You could try, but you're no match for me, if you ever were. They entrusted you to Persi, but still you pursue me. Only me. Not Persephone." She watched as his grin faded in fear at her cousin's name. Inspiration struck. "You signed over everything to her, didn't you? Your kind are big on written contracts. You gave her the shadows from your soul as part of the contract. You sealing such a bargain…summoned the storm."

He shrugged. "She can't wield my power without a bit of demon in her. I wasn't going to give her any other part of me. I gave it all up for you."

Renouncing everything for her. Redemption. Mel gasped, setting her cup down before she dropped it as realisation exploded in her mind. Redemption might be possible for him, and she knew how. "But it's not enough. You may have given up everything, but if you're truly after redemption, you'll need something a little more powerful than a peck on the cheek to complete the transformation. Is that really what you want, Luce?"

Luce clunked his cup on the table beside hers, sliding off the couch. He dropped to his knees on the rug, his hands out in supplication. "Please, Mel. Help me. I'm begging you. Finish what you started. I can't enter your world, yet I'm no longer a part of mine. Send me back or take me with you. Make me whole again and I'll do anything you ask."

Sixty-two

She stared down at the demon kneeling at her feet. She ached to help him, but to grant him the angel's kiss he asked for could hurt him more than she cared to. "I can't refuse to help you, but I don't know what will happen if I try. I might just banish you back to the Pit, where you'll stay for centuries until you can return."

Luce winked. "I'm willing to take the risk for one kiss from you. I promise I'll be good. Do my best not to corrupt you. Believe me when I say I don't want you to fall, Mel. Your kindness in letting me enter your house, when

I could harm you so easily…you're too trusting, but I owe you for that today. You'll make the best kind of angel, I know it. One day, I want to see how beautiful your wings will be."

"One day – will be?" Mel laughed so hard it took her almost a minute before she could continue, "You think I'm a fresh-faced Grigori, or an angel-in-training like Persi, waiting to earn my wings, and one kiss can corrupt me. Oh Hell – I really thought you'd have realised by now. Your soul is in far more danger than mine could ever be. Luce, look at me. Love isn't my weakness, but my strength." She rose to her feet, feeling all pretence of humanity slip away as her wings unfurled. Feathers brushed both the floor and the ceiling as her soul's normally concealed glow lit up the room. "If you wish to be like me, you must rise with me." She saw her radiance reflected in his eyes and ruthlessly reined it in before she overwhelmed him, but she also saw his eyes shine with hope. He wanted this. Truly, he did.

Luce stood up stiffly. "Mel…who are you? Your real name and rank, I mean. Like I'm

Lucifer, Light of the Morning. I was one of the Seraphim, until…" He swallowed. "You should know who I am before we go any further. I've never met an angel who could withstand me – and then, not for long."

She touched his arm, her sympathy overflowing. "I know your history, Luce. I witnessed it all from Earth, for my responsibilities keep me here," she said gently. "Just because you haven't met an angel stronger than you, doesn't mean we don't exist. In my true form, I am Muriel of the Hashmallim."

Luce stared at her, his mouth wide. He swallowed a few times before he laughed shakily. "A Domination? You're a Domination. The only female Domination, who I've never met. No wonder you managed to turn me down flat. I should have known."

Mel persisted. "I've known Earth and all its pleasures for longer than you have. You cannot corrupt me, but one kiss from me might destroy you, Luce. Are you willing to take that risk?"

"Hell's hot, but so are you. I'll take my

chances," Luce insisted. He licked his lips – Mel suspected out of nervousness more than lust. "You almost sound like you'd be sad if you destroyed me. Why did you enter my company and challenge me, if not to put an end to me?"

"I've always spent most of my time on Earth, dealing with leadership matters here. I guide and teach, not kill, Luce. You and your corporation were not aligned with my objectives." Mel bowed her head. Centuries of watching and guiding the leaders of her world gave her the strength she needed to try to redeem a demon. How much harder could it be?

"Close your eyes," she said softly. It wasn't necessary, but she was nervous and didn't want him watching her. It was, after all, her first time. No one she knew had ever redeemed a demon – it wasn't meant to be possible. She expected him to vanish in a burst of light as she banished him back to where his kind belonged. She didn't want to see the betrayal in his eyes if she failed, as she surely would.

But there was something different about

him…something that made her willing to take the chance. If this was what he truly wanted, then perhaps it was possible…

She drew closer, brushing her lips against his until she could feel his breath through his parted lips. He was correct – she would be saddened to send him home. Mel knew she was too kind-hearted for killing demons.

Drawing in a breath that tingled with jasmine, from his tea and hers, she tasted his lips. Sweeter and softer than she expected. Sharing air, skin and warmth, she gave him her tongue, too, trading it for his. A deep sound rumbled in his throat, but he didn't break their connection. Mel touched her fingers to his temples, wishing she could see his thoughts to know why. Was redemption worth so much to him, or was there more? She didn't want to hurt him.

Her lips sealed in his breath and she closed her eyes, too, as she opened her heart. Breathing her own spirit into him as part of a passionate kiss should have destroyed the salacious demon. Yet his arms closed carefully around her, a reverent embrace as he responded to her kiss.

So much sensation, touching far more than two bodies. In a kiss this deep, she felt the communion of two souls twining together – with no taint of corruption to darken the moment. She waited for him to fade from her arms as she sent him back to Hell, for the moment to end – but still their kiss continued. A true angel's kiss, so what did that make Luce?

She felt the spark of contact between her soul and his, igniting something in him that opened his heart to her. The flood of feeling from him swept away all illusions – she knew the depths of his soul and the intensity overwhelmed her.

A deafening explosion outside, accompanied by a bright burst of light, couldn't break the contact between them. The afterimage burned through Mel's eyelids even after her house was plunged into darkness.

Dimly, she became aware of the power in the house draining away. The refrigerator's hum silenced and the sole sounds were their shared breathing beneath the rain hissing down on the roof. The room was lit only by her golden glow. No – not anymore.

She'd turned a demon – and, possibly, blown the power transformer for the whole suburb in the process. She hoped the damage could be repaired – but it was a small price to pay for the redemption of a soul.

Mel pulled away, feeling the change as Luce began to give off light, too. Not as bright as Mel, but enough. "Luce, look," she said softly. "See what you've become."

He opened his eyes and looked down. "Thank you," Luce breathed. He flexed his fingers, the faint light from them shimmering in his eyes.

"How do you feel?" Mel asked, wondering what a redeemed demon was supposed to experience. She had no comparison. She allowed her radiance to dim into darkness, as she tried to focus on the faint connection she still seemed to have with his heart. When she faded, Luce was the only light in the room. A light she'd helped rekindle, which made him her responsibility.

"Some things are different, but some stay

the same. I still want you as much as ever. I almost wish you'd rejected me. The thought of taking you on the couch has turned from enticing to all-consuming. I want…more." He stared at her hungrily.

Mel took his arm, looking up to meet his eyes so he could read her soul if he wished. "Careful, or you'll wind up back in the Pit, right back where you started. Congress between angels and demons is forbidden, but two angels...Love is a very important part of life as an angel." She waited for her words to sink in.

"No, I'm sure I just want to seduce you out of your clothes so I can make love to you 'til morning." It took him a moment for his mind to catch up with his tongue. Luce looked shocked as he said, "I love you?" He shook his head hard. "No. Demons aren't capable of love. I can't love you. Unless…" Mel could see his eyes widening as he sensed it. "How did you do it? I do love you." The former demon's confusion was complete.

Mel laughed gently. "So it would seem." She leaned in close. "For future reference, I prefer

the bed to the couch — more space. Come."
She beckoned. "I don't want you to be alone
tonight. So, tell me, Luce. How good are you
in bed?"

Luce chuckled as he followed her. "I can
make an angel think she's in Heaven."

Sixty-three

Sunlight kissed her eyelids and Mel slipped out of bed.

Luce still slept soundly and she didn't want to wake him, so she left only a light kiss on the former demon's cheek. She padded quietly to the kitchen with her phone, lifted it and dialled. Two rings later, he answered.

"Hello?"

"Raphael, you know how you owe me a favour?"

The tale continues in

Mel Goes to Hell

ABOUT THE AUTHOR

Demelza Carlton has always loved the ocean, but on her first snorkelling trip she found she was afraid of fish.

She has since swum with sea lions, sharks and sea cucumbers and stood on spray drenched cliffs over a seething sea as a seven-metre cyclonic swell surged in, shattering a shipwreck below.

Demelza now lives in Perth, Western Australia, the shark attack capital of the world.

The *Ocean's Gift* series was her first foray into fiction, followed by her suspense thriller *Nightmares* trilogy. She swears the *Mel Goes to Hell* series ambushed her on a crowded train and wouldn't leave her alone.

Want to know more? You can follow Demelza on Facebook, Twitter, YouTube or her website, Demelza Carlton's Place at:

www.demelzacarlton.com

Books by Demelza Carlton

Siren of Secrets series

Ocean's Secret (#1)

Ocean's Gift (#2)

Ocean's Infiltrator (#3)

Siren of War series

Ocean's Justice (#1)

Ocean's Widow (#2)

Ocean's Bride (#3)

Ocean's Rise (#4)

Ocean's War (#5)

How To Catch Crabs

Nightmares Trilogy

Nightmares of Caitlin Lockyer (#1)

Necessary Evil of Nathan Miller (#2)

Afterlife of Alana Miller (#3)

Mel Goes to Hell series

The Devil's Work (#1)

See You in Hell (#2)

Mel Goes to Hell (#3)

To Hell and Back (#4)

The Holiday From Hell (#5)

All Hell Breaks Loose (#6)

The Devil Goes to Heaven (#7)

Romance Island Resort series

Maid for the Rock Star (#1)
The Rock Star's Email Order Bride (#2)
The Rock Star's Virginity (#3)
The Rock Star and the Billionaire (#4)
The Rock Star Wants A Wife (#5)
The Rock Star's Wedding (#6)
Maid for the South Pole (#7)
Jailbird Bride (#8)

Romance a Medieval Fairytale series

Enchant: Beauty and the Beast Retold
Dance: Cinderella Retold
Fly: Goose Girl Retold
Revel: Twelve Dancing Princesses Retold
Silence: Little Mermaid Retold
Awaken: Sleeping Beauty Retold
Embellish: Brave Little Tailor Retold
Appease: Princess and the Pea Retold
Blow: Three Little Pigs Retold
Return: Hansel and Gretel Retold
Wish: Aladdin Retold
Melt: Snow Queen Retold
Spin: Rumpelstiltskin Retold
Kiss: Frog Prince Retold
Reflect: Snow White Retold
Roar: Goldilocks Retold
Cobble: Elves and the Shoemaker Retold